THE MELODY THAT BINDS

C.M. DINSMORE

Paperback: 978-1-961421-00-4

Ebook: 978-1-961421-01-1

Hardcover: 978-1-961421-02-8

Audiobook available

Library of Congress Number: 2023938805

First edition v1.1

Originally published June 2023

Published in the United States by heliotropic.media

[HW100: This is a 100% human-written book]

Dedicated to Marco, Rick,
and the rest of their family

e pluribus unum

Contents

1945

Refuge

I scurry, grasping my rifle tight as it tries to break from my grip on each jolting step. Tips of outreaching foliage slap against me as I break through the reach of brittle branches. I swim through the sludge of warm air, smoke and dust irritating my eyes and nostrils. My mind races faster than my heart or feet. I stop, listen, and survey the sea of browning jungle. *Which way?* There, beyond the dried, thinned foliage is that peak, the one that caught my attention when I first chose to flee. *Ah yes*, an unmistakable marker. A towering rock, the sun glaring off its surface, shored up by the soft, flowing slopes leading to it. My thoughts condense into the sole objective as if tasked to follow a direct order.

My arms sting from the compounding scratches of the foliage. Each step, the mucus squished from my blisters lubricates the tight confines of my boots. The peak's beacon glares, and when hidden from view, I sense it behind the treetops. I glance behind me more often than I do at the peak. The jungle blankets me from the enemy's sight. I lean over, placing my hands above my knees to keep my chest and head high, laboring to catch my breath.

The last time I ran this hard and long, I did so with my best friend, Shiro, when we ran from Mr. Nakajima after setting his grass ablaze during our summer break. It was a one-mile sprint to Miyazawa Elementary, where we had completed third grade in the spring. We knew the school grounds well, having spent many days in the treeline that separated the school from the adjacent neighborhood. This arrowhead of trees was the entry point to the pathway that led up Mt. Takao, which we would venture farther and farther up each summer as we grew older.

"Don't climb the mountain," Shiro's parents would always remind us, up until the age of ten. "You'll get lost."

My father wasn't concerned. My mother's eyes would follow us each time we left with sharpened sticks made from fallen, misshapen tree branches. We referred to this treed area, starting at the school grounds and leading all the way up the mountain, as "Shima Territory." Shima Territory is where we chased, hid, and played war using our sticks as spears or rifles and rocks as grenades. Not until Shiro struck me above my right eye with his spear did we realize the danger of these objects. Shiro hung his head at the sight of the deep gash on my face. I explained to my mother that I ran into a branch protruding into the trail's path while she cleaned my wound with warm water and soap, her hiss of angst coming in place of any words. I didn't know if her disappointment was over seeing me injured or because she had to take time out of her day to tend to my injury. Shiro took it much more seriously than I did, but I suppose I would feel the same if I caused injury to him. But on that day we ran from Mr. Nakajima and arrived at Shima Territory, we both leaned over, placing our hands on our knees, gulping air like I do now.

Each breath slakes me as water would my thirst. Bang! The bullet slaps and cracks through the leaves and branches behind me. *This is real*, I say to myself, out from reverie and back to real weapons of war. I stand with the tip of my boot already angled and planted into the ground, ready to push off in a sprint. The jungle is quiet. My lack of breath quenched, I lift the tip of my boot out of the soil and take a soft step forward.

"Over there," a man shouts in an American accent.

My slow, cautious steps turn into a jog away from the voices. "This way," the American shouts.

They're close. I sprint away, gaining enough speed to glide through the jungle with little worry over the crunching and thud of my steps, leaping over rocks, balancing myself along the uneven ground, the branches slashing at me and insects bouncing off my face. A dragonfly gets caught in the trap of my opened mouth. I bring it closer to my lips with the tip of my tongue before ejecting it with a deep huff of breath and regaining the rhythm of my breathing. The men fanned out behind are like a wave ready to crash over me in a thalassic-like effect. Among the blur of my surroundings, which zip past, the canopy of trees opens. A new peak is revealed. I run towards it.

In the act of running away, I ponder, *honor or safety, country or self. Should I make one last stand? I'm worthy. I'm strong. A chance to prove myself before death.* The Bushido code sears into my consciousness. Guilt builds with each stride. I'm prepared to turn towards the enemy and shout "*Banzai*," as the word builds momentum within my gut. I'm encouraged further by the thought of dying a quick death by bullets and not at the hands of Filipinos who seek revenge. *Tamiko. Maeko.* The idea of a swift and honorable death is dashed away by the desire to see my wife and daughter again—whether or not they wish to see me.

Tamiko's parents allowed her a day off from working at her family's livestock feed store. I took Tamiko to the small lake where Shiro and I found our new clubhouse weeks before. It was an abandoned hut with weather-darkened wood and bamboo. I learned she wanted to be a veterinarian. On her suggestion, we built an animal hospital—at least that's what she called it—in the corner of the hut, made from recycled bamboo and wood. We couldn't gather any animals and instead collected plants and insects. We already had a supply of makeshift tools, including a pipe as a hammer and nails we pulled from used wood. We placed the different plants and insects we collected into the cage; that's what I'd call her hospital. To no surprise, the insects didn't hang around long, crawling over the edge of the box or through the gaps of our patchwork of wood. Even the plants poked out through the opening, as if making their escape. Her parents demanded she return by dusk, but as we prepared to leave, she pointed to the green light of the fireflies along the stream that flowed into the lake. "Look," she said, after we had already returned all the plants and insects into the wild and tidied up the hut for the next person.

We sat in the very spot where we'd stopped upon seeing the fireflies and watched their dancing lights. I looked over to Tamiko, her eyes jumping from firefly to firefly and a broad grin lighting up her face. While she stared at the fireflies, I looked at her until she looked over to me. I was summoning the courage to lean in and kiss her lips or cheek, depending on what was easier to reach.

"Thank you for inviting me, friend" she said, as if sensing what was on my mind.

I turned away, back towards the fireflies, as if the disappointment on my face was visible in the darkness. I didn't say much on the walk home, wondering what I could have done differently. She didn't say much either, concerned about her curfew.

Although her parents didn't allow her a day off again that summer, they allowed me to visit. Our friendship grew. I knew that when the time was right, I'd try for a kiss again. It wasn't until a much-delayed moment, three summers later, that her parents allowed her to spend the day with me away from their property.

It was that summer, after years of courting other girls, when I had the choice between asking her what she thought about me or bypassing all of that and going for the kiss. We sat along the riverbank at the back of her property when a similar moment to our first date presented itself and we were surrounded by the glow of fireflies again. I took it as a sign and looked over to her, fixated on the fireflies. The upcurve of her smiling lips leveled off when she felt my gaze upon her. She turned to look into my eyes. Sensing no words on the tip of her tongue, I leaned in. She leaned towards me, giving me confidence to go further and kiss her on the lips. The kiss lasted two seconds. I went back to my original position, reeling from the adrenaline, and having no doubts about how she felt. We turned back to gaze at the fireflies, and she laid into me with our arms and shoulders touching. My body tingled, and anything in life seemed possible. We were comfortable in our silence.

The next time I saw her, she said, "My father asked me to invite you for dinner tomorrow."

"Umm..."

"It'll be ok, Kaiyo," she said, squeezing my wrist with both hands.

Despite my parents never saying or doing anything to stall Tamiko and my friendship-turned-relationship, I was bound by the obligation to them. Year after year, my father stacked more duties onto me. I escaped by joining the army before I turned eighteen, in preparation for starting a new life with Tamiko. The night before proposing to her, I visited Tamiko's parents, Mr. and Mrs. Yoshida, after Tamiko's bedtime. I waved to Mr. Yoshida through the window to get his attention, not wanting to wake Tamiko by knocking on the door. He opened the door but did not greet me with a smile. When I looked over to Mrs. Yoshida standing behind him, she did greet me with her normal smile.

"I heard you joined the army?" he said, after opening the door.

"Yes, sir," I answered.

"It's been hard on Tamiko. She's been in her room all day after hearing the news."

"I'm sorry, sir."

"When do you leave for training?"

"Two weeks from today." I began my next sentence with "Sir," and he invited me in.

I sat down with Mr. and Mrs. Yoshida and asked for their blessing to have Tamiko's hand in marriage.

Mrs. Yoshida responded with, "But you'll be away, Kaiyo. Are you sure this is the best decision?" her hands remaining on her lap and a slight tilt to her head.

"I have no doubts I want to be with Tamiko. I love her. If you don't think she wants to be with me or should be with me, then I understand."

"She would never forgive us if we didn't allow this," Mrs. Yoshida said, her head straightening, looking over to Mr. Yoshida as if the affirmation of my love for Tamiko reminded her of their own love story.

The next day, Mr. and Mrs. Yoshida had convinced Tamiko to meet me at the lake near our clubhouse, where we once sat looking at the fireflies on what I considered our first date. I didn't have time to wait for this year's fireflies, and we sat under a purple-orange evening sky.

She was upset on arrival and unable to look at me. "Why didn't you tell me?"

"I'm sorry, Tamiko. I should have told you," I said.

I wanted to tell her "to escape my parents," but openly criticizing my parents wasn't respectable behavior.

"You're leaving me," she said to me with a deflated face.

"This wasn't easy for me," I told her.

Tamiko looked down, attempting to hide her building emotions. I reached for her arm, and she pulled away from me. I reached out again, grabbing her hand.

"Be my wife?"

She looked up and stared at me with eyes glistening with pent-up tears. "Will you be my wife?" I asked again.

She placed her hand over her mouth, looked away, and was silent. "Tamiko? I love you," I said, my body flushed with fear, thinking I had lost her forever.

I pulled on her arm, urging her to face me.

She whipped around in my direction. "Yes," she said, barely audible and nodding, then removing her hand from her mouth. "Yes," she said clearly, leaning into me and resting her head on my chest.

The cold of fear throughout my body turned warm, and no other moment in life since has lifted my spirit as high.

We married 19 December 1940 in a small wedding at her family's home. One of the last conversations Tamiko and I had before starting basic training was about children. There were many times I made comments during our time together as friends and partners that painted a picture for her of my position. "If you can't love the child fully and provide for them, then it's better not to have them," I told her, jaded from my own relationship with my parents.

I believe she thought I never wanted children, which was true until the day I decided to propose to her and saw bearing a child as the pinnacle of consummating my love for her.

"Maybe we can have a child when you get back," she said, not looking up at me while helping me pack.

"If you promise to give me a future judo champion or baseball star," I replied, as a joke.

She looked up and smiled in the biggest smile I had ever seen from her, glowing. I think she already knew of her pregnancy during our talk but informed me in a letter a month later.

"I'll do what I can," she said, laughing.

My goodbye to Shiro was succinct. "I may be right behind you," he said in parting.

"Don't join," I told him. "Don't join because I joined."

"I don't think I'll have much choice," he said.

My instincts returning, I'm drawn to my right, up a slight incline, and away from the new peak. I run with more resolve towards what I know and don't see than in the direction of the peak I do see. I run as the wave of pursuers channels through the contour of the lower valley and past me. The gradual incline of an increasing slope slows my pace as I look down at my feet to guide each earned step. I scan around for a dark hole to crawl into. My adrenaline spent and legs near collapse under my body's weight, I stop to catch my breath. *What next?* I look up above the trees to find my peak.

Relying on will, I climb and dodge the hanging branches as if I'm avoiding the swinging arms of the enemy. I ascend above the smog of scorched air from weeks of intense gunfire and explosions. In the cool, pure air that reaches my skin, I breathe in the sweetness of flowering plants diluted by peat.

> *The last time I remember the smell of flowers was when Maeko raised a light-pink, ruffled carnation to my nose. I sniffed. Maeko smiled at me while the sweet, spicy fragrance reached deep into my nostrils. I could not smile back, as much as I wanted to. She brought the flower to her nose and sniffed in curiosity or simply to mimic her father.*
>
> *The last time I smelled the peatiness of the earth this distinctly was days before fleeing while hunkered down in retreat within a freshly dug foxhole as the passing bullets whizzed above me. My nose was pressed hard against the soil and churned-up peat amid the prospect of an imminent death.*

The ordinary smell of peat today is as sweet as Maeko's carnation then. The thick foliage on both sides funnels me up the slope until I reach a rock wall twice my height. I toss my rifle and knapsack onto the ridge above and find contours along the rock wall to latch my fingers into, and insert the tips of my tattered leather boots before hoisting myself onto the ledge. I roll onto my back, exhausted. Pointed rocks press into my flesh as if they dig for my kidneys. *Let me rest,* I beg. The shouting and gunshots echo in the valley below all afternoon in fading and resurging commotion. A separate wave of pursuers comes into range.

"This way," someone shouts.

The voices fade into mumbles. I take a deep breath before turning to my side and towards the peak, expecting the challenge of another steep climb to show itself. A barrier of thick trees and bushes crowd my sight, so closely bunched they don't provide any gaps to see beyond. I lift my sights above the barrier to see only blue sky. An unproductive thought enters my mind for the first time since the battle began. An orchard, a lake, and reunion with comrades play to my optimism over what may be on the other side. *Tetsu. Hansuke. Are they alive?* If any of my fellow soldiers survived, I'd be riddled with gunshots before they could know it was me.

The sharp edges of the rocks prod, reminding me of my father poking me awake on a much too early morning to fetch tobacco for his *kiseru*. And just as I couldn't ignore the demands of my father, I can't ignore the rock nudging me to get up. I jump to my feet, pick up my rifle, and dive into the wall of vegetation while closing my eyes and holding my breath. The incline is slight, and the vegetation thins after a few yards of fighting through the snagging tentacles of the bushes. I exhale as I break through to the other side and brush the bits of dry leaves and branches off my face before opening my eyes. The sun gleams off the sandy soil, obscuring sight of whatever lies ahead, and as a breeze blows the baking sand onto me, my eyes adjust to the brightness to reveal, like the curtain dropping in kabuki theatre on a paradisiacal setting, the nook. It is carved out of the side of the mountain in a near-perfect wedge, and bursting with fauna. Birds dance around me, swoop through the air, and sing as though excited by my presence. The small light-brown yellowish ones with white bellies are most abundant, intermingling with the smaller bright yellow canary-like ones. Their two colors weave a flash of a threaded, yellow-brown ribbon as they streak from tree to tree. The sharper pitch of the small ones rises above all the other sounds, piercing my ears in contrast to the booms and pops that I have mistaken for normality. *Oasis. How do I find myself here?* I hold my hand in front of my face, playing with my fingers. *Am I dreaming?* Gunshots from the valley remind me I'm not. I'm isolated from the battlefield but not safe from those who hunt me. I'm in a dangerous game of hide-and-seek where there's a severe consequence in being found, unlike the childhood war games in *Shima Territory*.

The barrier of foliage lines the edge of the nook, enclosing me in a half-circle. A slice into the mountainside makes a rear-rock-wall that blocks me in unless I traverse around the wall and up the steep mountain slope. The trees and bushes fight for space along the barrier, where the dirt is most fertile and not choked by the sandy soil from the weathered rock of the rear-rock-wall. Aside from the frenzied growth along the barrier, my island of a nook is filled with a modest spread of trees and plants, peppered with boulders, and dotted with grassy plots.

Moths, beetles, and mosquitoes flutter and buzz around me, masking the drone of planes circling the valley. I'm faced with a new set of challenges as the initial grandeur of the nook provides a short break for my eyes, nose, and ears after being drenched in war. The sense of peace is drained from my face when reality hits me. *I'm being hunted!* This nook is a dead-end unless I climb farther up the mountain only to expose myself or return to the valley below, making it easier for the enemy to track me. The "dead" in dead-end looms large. *I must wait it out. Wait them out.*

Walking toward the rear-rock-wall, searching for cover, I'm greeted by an old tree standing out in height, girth, and the complex intertwining of its thick branches, as if it is an orgy of petrified pythons. The tree shields a dark hole at the base of the rear-rock-wall. *A tunnel that goes straight through the center of the mountain,* I think, as my imagination inflates my hope for escape. I walk past the old tree to see that the hole is no cave, but a den made up of two slabs of rock leaning against each other like sumo wrestlers in a standing draw. The rear-rock-wall behind is dark gray, smooth solid rock with faded-green moss brushed over the surface like water paint that has soaked into the paper it was painted on.

I stick my head through the opening to inspect the den. Light from a cleft above seeps through at the rear, where the slabs meet the rear-rock-wall, illuminate the arrangement inside. The den's floor is a welcoming smooth sand with wavy patterns of mud at the back created by water trickling down the wall and collecting in the den. I'm uneasy on entry, like an animal lured into a trap. *Too good to be true.* I lean in and poke every corner of the den. The ruckus from the valley and the continued buzz in the air nudge me to waste no more time concealing myself. I crawl into the den through the triangular entrance, coughing on the cloud of dust caused by disturbing the dry soil. I hold my breath, and as I wait for the dust cloud to clear, notice the tremble in my right hand, the slouch of my posture, tightness of my jaw, and my vice-like grip on the rifle. I peel my warm, sweaty hands from the metal and set down my rifle. The air cleared, I breathe deep before clasping my hands together and squeezing hard. The trembling shoots up both arms as though the other arm has joined the *oshi* of a *bonshō*.

"Come on," I say, as I clasp harder. "Stop."

Weak. Coward. I look up through the cleft to gauge the sun's position. The large body of a yellow-black spotted spider blocks my view, its web strung out over the opening, any sense of danger masked by its familiarity.

Shiro approached them with caution.
"Don't get bitten," is all he would say when I held them, as they crawled up my rotating hand and arm.
Holding up a spider in Shiro's face, similar to the one which shares my den, I said, "Look, no fangs," while petting it with one finger across its large, glossed, ceramic-like body.
My curiosity guided my adventurous escapes. If I stayed around the farm exploring after finishing my duties or remained in an otiose state of daydream, my father would eventually call out orders. Autonomy on the farm and daydreaming until content were a luxury.

Picking up the rifle, I guard the entrance to the den, peering back into the jungle as if doing so is a courageous act. Those valley echoes fade to silence as dusk settles in. I'm slow and intentional in my movement, coming out of my crouch with the circulation not yet returned to my limbs, and lie flat on my back. I continue to clench the rifle with chafed hands. My thoughts race with all the different ways I will be found or killed once asleep. *A grenade rolling into the den and blowing me to pieces* is what I settle on. *A quick death.*

A new awareness of my aching, dry throat is brought on by the dripping down the rear-rock-wall. I pop open the canteen and drink with the indelicacy of cotton ball-like, chapped lips, and I'm unable to stop myself until the partially-filled canteen is empty. I crawl over to catch the dripping water in the cup of my cheek before swallowing what little collects. I do this for several minutes before placing the canteen under the drip and lying back down. The drops alternate between plopping into and slapping against the outside of the canteen from two separate drip paths.

The den's slanted slabs conceal me well, and my breathing calms in sync with the gradual change of the jungle shadows and the cooling air. Nighttime arrives. The drip-drop of water acts as metronome to the crickets and frogs. With the rifle resting across my chest, I stare into the vast mystery of the jungle. Man, beast, spirits all take turns leaping from the darkness. The moonlight saves me from my imagination, outlining the canopy of trees and gleaming onto my face through the cleft. The crepuscular serves as a dramatic nocturne. The impenetrable rock slabs serve as bodyguards. Only then do I rid myself of the spider dangling over my body, by knocking it to the ground with my rifle and tossing it far out from the den by flipping it with the tip of my boot.

"Don't come back," I tell it. *The den is mine.*

> *My bedroom at the farm was the only other time I had my own space. I was twelve when I charged out of my room one evening and demanded they "knock before entering, and don't go into my room unless I say you can. Look at what you did," as I held up the haiku which I had spent days writing, deliberate and thoughtful, on the cleanest piece of white paper I could find. It had a muddy footprint across it.*
>
> *I braced myself for one of them to counter with criticism of my harsh tone but walked away when I realized that if I stood there long enough one or both of them would respond.*

In the lull of night, I twitch to each rustle and snap. I shiver from a steady breeze, and with it a wary peace from the night's own natural rhythm and the distant commotion of war. Frogs croak, crickets chirp, bats flap against the moonlit sky, trees sway as if caught in the ebb and flow of a tide, varmints dig through the dry leaves on the ground, mosquitoes hover near my head, and a constant hiss fills the air. I hear nature's own song chords as if tuning up to play a melody, and feel untethered for the first time since the start of the war.

"You're the property of Japan. That means, as your superior, I own you," Captain Mori said.

Prior to this, our officers would tell us, "You are protecting Japan's and your family's honor. You are protecting our great emperor."

Captain Mori's approach was less inspiring, but more honest. He earned my respect for speaking truth in his introduction to our company. All those years of my father's harsh criticisms and commands prepared me for Captain Mori.

I stood looking over at a group of soldiers digging a foxhole in the line of fire of another group's foxhole, and prepared to inform the soldiers of their error, when Captain Mori stepped up next to me.

"Do you think you can lead these idiots someday?" he asked me, as we stood watching.

"Yes sir," I responded, as a matter of routine, taking the question as a rhetorical one.

He charged towards the guilty group. "Are you trying to win the war for the Americans?"

At the time, I was a Superior Private. Three weeks later, I found myself Lance Corporal and leading a platoon after their former leader, Masao, vanished after a direct hit by a mortar. I suppose it made it easier for his—now my—platoon that Masao's maimed, lifeless body didn't lie there reminding them of the horror we found ourselves in. He disappeared, as if him being there was part of our collective imagination. The was no evidence he was ever there, including the mention of his name.

The sharp pitch of memories from war drowns out any noise from the jungle, wrestling and forever pinning me to its reality. It pokes and stabs at me—the shouting, the screaming, the booms, the pops all filling my mind's ear. The stench of unsanitary living and rotting bodies infects the walls of my nostrils. The bloodstained ground, with its mangled bodies, has scorched the mucus of my eyeballs. Unforgiving truths snap at the heels of the fickle hope brought on by this new refuge. I readjust my body on each nagging thought, then mumble in the weariness of near-sleep. The moon has shifted each time I look up through the cleft, as a restless night endures. Thoughts of life back in Japan find their way to me in flashes, as childhood memories fight for recognition, trying to quell my mind's turmoil over war. I tug these pleasant memories to the surface.

My childhood home, was a small solitary bamboo farmhouse on the outskirts of Hiroshima, surrounded by the clean lines of rice paddies. The lines between nature and civilization blurred. Takao peak rose in the background and waves of smaller mountains crashed up against it. Memory of my mother carrying me up the driveway is vivid. I believe this memory marked my first arrival to the farm after birth when only a baby; but common sense tells me otherwise. I often relive the gentle bounce of her footsteps while wrapped warm between the soft cloth that lie across my forehead. The loose ends of hanging thread tickling my face as moth-

er's warmth seeps through the cloth comforted me then and in reminiscence today. Ominous shapes of the mountains stand tall beyond the fog of an early morning arrival as the mist collects like tiny fish eggs on her jet-black hair and the cloth that covers me. I'm there. I'm here. A manufactured reality perhaps.

Ah yes, softening my face as my mind bathes in childhood memories before memories of war roar back for attention and drown any pleasant thoughts. The haunting precedes the fears of my present situation. Then, the weight of my eyelids dulls my sense of worry. The heaviness brings me to surrender to the night. Failing to conjure the spirit of Bushido and hold on to those rational concerns of survival, I find myself between consciousness and sleep. The irrationality of my emerging oneiric subconscious moves in like a dense cloud as my mind catches pace with an exhausted body. I fall deep into sleep. Buried thoughts resurface in a morphed dream state, only to recycle recent horrors with my distant past and contentious present into a wicked unified narrative. Nightmares where my family appear next to me in battle, soldiers and civilians that were maimed by gunshots and explosions visit me on the childhood farm on which I grew up, and as we're all surrounded by a jungle abyss. They all show up trying to help me find a way home. A consortium of desultory thoughts in the mind's effort to reconcile who I am, was, and will become.

New World

Day 1

The battlefield roars with darting action as I huddle deep within a foxhole and bullets whizz overhead. The silhouette of a man stands over me, the sun's glare filling the background. The man leaps into the foxhole and grabs a handful of my uniform. He yanks me to my feet. It's my father. He looks down at me, and then his face disappears in a shifting stance that blocks the sun and recreates the silhouette of his large frame. I cover my eyes, anticipating the sun splashing into my vision on his next shift in stance, but when I peek between my fingers my father's silhouette is transferred to the rice paper walls of my childhood home. His silhouette grows as I hear my mother play the koto. *The sweet and soothing melody warms me to a ticklish shiver. My father slides open the door in the room next to me, where*

> *my mother plays. The hard edges of their shadows flicker in the candlelight. My mother pauses, and the tip of her nose points up towards my father. His voice rumbles, harsh and direct. My father walks away, leaving the door open. My mother continues playing. The melody reverberates through the house. The glare of the candle intensifies, fading out my mother's silhouette. The candle's heat strikes my face, the burn now resonates from a flamethrower as I'm brought back to the battlefield. The soldier next to me throttles the trigger while aiming at a* nipa *hut. Familiar screams come from within where the voices and faces of everyone I know jumble together. The heat pulls me away from the friends, family, and comrades in my convoluted dream.*

The burn jerks me out from sleep. I squint to the sun shining through the cleft and across my face, wiping the plight of those familiar voices and faces from thought. I shield my face with one arm, my trembling hand inches from my eye, while the other arm hugs the rifle. If I were back home in Japan staring at the outlines of Mt. Takao below the orange-purple clouds at sunset immersed in sublime thoughts, I think these trembling hands would still curse me. I have no memory of gazing at the sunset here despite the many evenings watching over the landscape.

"Banzai!" I say, jolting myself out from unproductive thoughts. *I must survive this day.*

My eyes canvas the den before a plop summons me to check on the can- teen. I crawl over to it, drink the collected water, then place it back down to collect more water. The small amount of water does little to remedy my sandpaper-like tongue and aching throat. As I start to feel the muddling effects of dehydration, my inner voice becomes simple and concise. *Survive.*

Having slept the entire night in my uniform, I remove my boots and peel off my blood-stained socks, worn through at the heels.

"Hai," I say, as the cool air meets my hot, throbbing feet.

All the other pains of my body disappear, like if receiving a shot of morphine. As the relief wears off, the sting of my arms and legs from all the scratches and cuts returns. The triangle-shaped entrance frames the sea of trees and the rocky peaks of the adjacent mountain range on the other side of the valley. The distance reinforces my sense of safety in seclusion. *But I will need fire soon.*

The first time Shiro and I reached Takao Peak, I peered in the direction of the farm searching for the rectangles of our rice paddies and that meandering creek behind.
"Do you see it?" I asked Shiro.
Shiro peered alongside me. Our eyes scanned the landscape, eager to be the first to spot the farm.
"There," Shiro's finger shot out. "You were looking too far north."
"Ah ok, I see," I told him, even though I hadn't yet located the farm.
As we gazed over the landscape and ate dried cuddle fish Shiro's mother had packed for him, I located the creek and followed until I saw the glare of sunlit chrome from my father's motorcycle. "Do you think they can see us?" asked Shiro.
"Of course not."
"Maybe if we send smoke signals, they will know it's us."
"Your parents might notice. Not mine," said I.

Water. I stand the rifle next to the entrance of the den and subitize the items inside the knapsack. There are twenty bullets, one grenade, and a green apple found in an abandoned American foxhole days earlier. I set the apple on top of the knapsack and thought of its sourness tensing up the back of my tongue. *I must resist and save for later.* My eyes peruse for familiar round, oval, or oblong shapes among the treetops, as finding my next meal would give me permission to eat the apple. The snaps, cracks, and persistent hiss pin me within the den. I question whether the sounds are real or tricks of the mind. My mind, coming in and out of the muddle, struggles to decide on actions for survival. *Fire. Water. Food. Rest.*

My busy eyes find details within the nook missed yesterday. There's a diversity of trees and bushes where no two are the same in size, color, or type, yet holding an essential likeness. Small stair-like niches on the rear-rock-wall are packed with more bushes and small trees. I am far below the mountain's distinctive sharp peak. The old tree stands in front of the den's entrance, its branches filtering out the sun for most of the day. A large, flat-surfaced elongated rock slab, which looks like a table, sits exposed on the sandy soil. The den, tree, and rock-table an equal distance apart from each other. I can't help to think how convenient the table will be if I find food and amused by that thought since I may never find food. *Water,* I remind myself. *I'm losing my mind.*

I drink the collected water from the canteen in one gulp, hoping to lubricate my mind and delay insanity. It's been a week since I had a proper drink, surviving on the rationing of my canteen during the final battle. What little water was taken-in over the last day perspired out twofold, and that's without any labor. *I am samurai,* a thought used as a child to boost my confidence. A product of reading *The Book of Five Rings* at the age of nine after falling in love with reading at six years old. The artwork of a samurai on the cover caught my attention. The aggressive stance of the warrior on the cover, which I later learned represents author

Miyamoto Musashi, is seared into my mind as masculine, confident, heroic. I recite, "I am samurai," digging deep for the rumble in my voice. It's as if memories of my life flash before me in bits and pieces, while a slow, immanent death approaches. *Can't change the past. Can't change the past.* Forward-thinking eludes me. *No. No. It's dehydration. I need water. That's all. Water.*

"Kaiyo," I call to myself, rattling my head from side to side as though it will clear my mind and bring me an increased sense of urgency.

> *"What did you study at the university," Captain Mori asked me on the day he awarded me my Lance Corporal insignia.*
> *"University, sir?"*
> *"Didn't you attend university?" "I did but never finished," I told him.*
> *"But you're more educated than anyone in the company. You shared the history of the Philippines. You told how the Spanish once conquered this land when you were comparing Spanish words and names with Tagalog words and names."*
> *"I like to read, sir. My education was reading more than I ever would in college. Mostly Japanese books. But to expand my English vocabulary I read an entire English dictionary. Multiple times."*
> *"Ha," he responds. "I went to one of the best universities and am no more educated than you." He grins at me. "We never learned of the Spanish conquering this part of the world."*
> *"But it helped you become an effective commander. A doer," I explained.*
> *I was eager to tell him more about this land we found ourselves in or share a haiku with him.*

"Open your hand."
I opened my hand, and he slapped the two wing-like stripes into my open hand.
"Make me proud," he told me.

I sit all day scanning the trees, watching, listening in a passive use of my senses, at times visualizing about food as I once did about women. Those small-yellow canaries swoop and jump from branch to branch in herky-jerky, toy-like movement. *Who, what created you?* My fecund thoughts expand to the trees, then the mountains, and that bright orb in the sky, all peculiar in artificialness. *Water. Before long, I'll hallucinate.* The drip-drop of water rises above all else. I wait. I count. *I'll drink at twenty. One.* I wait. A buzz. I wait. A chirp. I wait. *Is Maeko eating well?* I wait. The jungle hisses. A snap. *Is she safe? Two.*

A maringouin buzzes above me after entering through the cleft. I'm on high-alert, with capture by my enemies paramount in my thoughts again. Out of all the noises, the mosquito's buzz is closest to the drone of a plane. *Survive, Water*, I remind myself. I suck the small amount of collected water from the canteen after counting nine drops. My tongue absorbs it all and none reaches my throat.

The angle of the sunlight outlines the rounded, dark shape of a coconut buried deep within the line of trees at nook's edge. Sight of this jostles my growing atrophy. I stick my head out of the den to get a better look, while attributing a steady bombinate to my psychosis. I shake my head and clear each ear with my finger before concentrating on the sound as it gets louder. A plane veers around the side of the mountain. I pull my head back into the den and peek out of the cleft to see the blur of its rigid, dark-green metal as the plane flies over me. The plane, with the big white star on its side flashing in the momentary glare of the sun's light, dips into the valley. Any thought of leaving the den, climbing up the tree, and retrieving that coconut, evaporates. *A noose of soldiers tightens around the mountain*, I imagine. *The plane's flyover is the last attempt at intel before the assault.*

"Banzai," I say, summoning energy in preparation for a final stand.

Afternoon arrives. My posture slouches and eyes gloss over as the heaviness of heat and lost hope weighs on me. I lie down and fixate on the drip-drop of the water falling into the canteen and snack on passing insects. *Where's all the real food? Fruit. Meat. That coconut,* I remember. My hebetude tames the tremble in my right hand as the cool evening breeze rattles the leaves. The sun leaves a swath of soft evening light at the entrance, like a doormat, and the smell of hot stone flows through the den.

> *It was a Sunday morning when I woke to a quiet morning all to myself. My parents departed early, while I slept, to attend the wedding of the daughter of my father's friend. That morning, despite an opportunity to sleep in, I woke at my usual time with the routine to do so ingrained in me. My duties on the farm waited for me. I lay there, with the breeze blowing through the cherry blossom tree near my window and the sun painting a triangle at the foot of my bed. The smell of* sakura, *mud, and grass; usually hidden by the scent of my mother's tea, made it to me as I lay in bed. I worked harder than I ever did that day, and finished my duties early, simply to return to my bed and lie there late in the afternoon, daydreaming about scenarios where my parents never returned. They returned late that evening.*

I lie with rifle resting across my chest, barrel pointed towards the entrance, and bayonet readied to thrust into any marauding face which might peek in the den. I stare into the darkness of the jungle, an auroral glow in the background giving a menacing presence to the old tree, the peculiar sounds of the night unsettling as the jungle encroaches on my comfort in a new sense of nyctophobia. The old tree creeks as if to warn the jungle from intruding our space. I try reaching slumber before my mind dives into the turmoil of a haunted subconscious. Jaws tight, eyelids heavy, I find my way to sleep amid the ebb and flow of my mind.

Day 2

Leeches cover me under my soaking-wet uniform. Their sanguivorous suckle squeezes against the surface of my skin. "Snake!" The foxhole next to us splatters and splash with the soldiers' panic. These noises and the intermittent popping of distant gunshots interfere with the hush of night. The anxious new recruit next to me, his face hidden in the dark, drowns me with words by reciting his life story.

"Did I tell you I lived on a farm?" he asks, repeating the question every so often and adding another detail about his life each time. The stories are familiar.

The sky lights up with a bursting flare. I look over at the young soldier in the flutter of orange light from the falling flare. The confusing shadows create the illusion that the recruit's face is deformed. Looking closer, he is a younger version of me I suppose. An odd sensation to look at a self which is me and not me. He holds a frown, as if disappointed that I see him. The sleeve of his uniform extends over one hand. The other hand carries a stick for a rifle.

"Father?" He looks to me for guidance.

A raindrop splashes on his cheek, and when more raindrops fall, the frown turns to a smile with the gloss of his skin reflecting the moonlit sky. The boy jumps out of the hole. I follow. We run into the jungle splashing each other as we stomp through the puddles and race towards a clearing ahead. It opens into a rice field and on the other side of the paddy is my childhood home. The boy runs through the flooded fields, waving me on to follow.

"Come on," he says.

I jump into the flooded field, and the resistance of the water slows me. My smile levels-off when the water is up to my waist. The boy disappears into my childhood home, but I'm no closer to it. The water rises to my neck, then my mouth. I'm paralyzed, swallow water, choke.

I wake with water dripping into my mouth from the cleft above. A soot-like cloud passes over, in view through the opening. There's a distant rumble and leaves rattle to a gust of wind.

Water! I exit the den and look up towards the sky. Another cloud among many scattered clouds filters the sun, and the spray of shattered droplets whirl in the wind. I wait with hands drawn towards the sky as though I'm caught in a moment of spiritual ascension. Mouth open and eyes closed, I wait. Opening one eye, I peek at the gray sky. The first succulent drop thuds onto my face. I close my eyes. Rain slaps onto my face and the leaves around me. The rhythm of the few is lost in the eventual slosh of the many. My face sleek-wet and mouth filling with water, I gulp, then open wide again. I collect and swallow three more times, with an aftertaste from the filth washed from my skin leaving a growing bitterness on my tongue with each gulp. The rain stops. The cloud passes. I'm drenched. The trailing mist cools the air as the sun shines bright again, creating a rainbow in the distance.

My skin is first to dry. I'm energized, my worried frown momentarily gone. Water trickles off the trees and rocks. The jungle hisses much like when water cools the hot stones of a sauna. The freshness of a rinsed jungle provides a short break from the overload of scents. The birds re-emerge, chirping and hitting their notes. Wet surfaces evaporate before my eyes as if time has sped up. Streams of water, delayed from their meandering journey down the mountain, cascade down the rear-rock-wall. I stand under one stream of flowing water outside the den with my mouth wide-open.

"Water," I gasp, "Water."

A few more days of life just as some of the plants around me would say.

Moving into the stream of falling water, I rub my scalp to loosen the filth of dirt, twigs, and bugs held within the thick net of my tangled hair, which smells of smoke and gunpowder. The water runs down my body, leaving a hint of red from all my cuts and scratches within the brownish puddle at my feet. I remove and toss my tattered shirt and pants, with their thin thousand-stitch waistband, onto the slant of the den wall. A thousand- stitch waistband is stitched one stitch at a time by family and friends and given to all departing soldiers. It was given to me by Tamiko.

"Even your parents sewed a stitch," she told me.

Liberated by nudity, I scrub hard, at times peeling off layers of dirt with my fingernails as if I'm shedding a snakeskin.

"Hai," I say, renewed from the rainfall.

I wash my clothes by rubbing together the fabric under the weakening stream of water. The friction releases excess dirt. I stop rubbing when the water dripping from the shirt turns clear, which is about the same time the stream of water turns to a trickle. I lay my clothes over bushes to dry, as the branches spread the fabric out like does the bamboo frame of a rice-paper lantern.

> *Mother dried clothes on azalea bushes next to our cherry blossom tree. I found the peace and inspiration from the soft-pink cherry blossoms greeting me for school on sunny mornings during spring. I didn't despised learning or my classmates, but it felt like I was missing out on something outside the four man-made walls of our schoolhouse. Many days I stared out of the classroom window towards the mountains, imagining what adventures await me. Sensing that freedom out there.*

My mind lubricated, I gather my thoughts before my judgement is clouded. *Dry clothes, coconut*; accounting for my two immediate priorities. I walk over to the coconut tree and look up. I hop onto the base of the tree and the rough tree bark scratches against my nude body. I jump off and wipe off the dusty, tree-bark residue. I return to my drying clothes, flip them over, and spread them out wider that the tips of the branches nearly poke through the fabric. *Hurry. Dry.* The camouflaged garments dry under the loose canopy of the nook. *No planes*, as I look up to the sky.

I wait and sift out a drone from the constant bombinate in the air before putting on my drying clothes and hopping onto the tree. I shuffle myself up the tree but make little progress, sliding down as much as I move up. I hug the tree, waiting for my next move. In the silence, and as I look up to the sole coconut, my attention turns to a hum. *A plane, a bug, my paranoia?* Waiting for the answer, my clutch on the tree weakens. The bombinate gets louder. *Plane!* I hop off and sprint towards the den, its entrance the finish line. I jump over rocks and bushes, closing in on the triangle opening, and I glimpse the tip of the plane's wing coming from around the mountain ridge. I leap into the den, clipping my back on the entrance. The collision knocks the breath out of me. I roll over in pain from the collision, grunting, and turning myself around to mark the position of the sunlight coming through the cleft with a twig.

Mosquitoes pester me in a swarming frenzy, brought to life by the splash of rain. Then quicker than they appeared, they disappear as another gust of wind blows through. Clouds gather above. A light mist swirls with the wind. Those heavy raindrops remain pent-up in the clouds above the nook as rain falls on the adjacent mountain range. *It's their turn.* The dark-gray drape beyond is like a well-composed dramatic scene from a Kenji Mizoguchi film. I wash the grime from all sores on my feet with water from my canteen and prop my feet on top of the knapsack to dry them. The breeze soothes, nearly putting me to sleep. Stomach pangs snap me out of the indulgence.

The moonlight replaces twilight, and the flutter of bats replace the swoosh of birds. The nighttime coolness from a cloud of serein blows through the den, emboldening my lethargy. My limbs surrender to gravity and rest firm on the ground. Aside from reverie and dreams, my less-welcomed nightmares take me away from the reality of my present. *Tamiko. Maeko. Shiro.* The brief moments of seeing the faces of those important to me are worth the haunting that pollutes these pleasant images—at least on some nights. Faces among mangled bodies of Filipinos along the roadside swoop in and out of my mind's eye. *Who are you?* I wonder, with each unnamed face. It's the empty void of the pupils surrounded by the off-white of decay that sears me. *Who were you?* My eyes weigh heavy. Dreading what's to come in sleep, I'm saved by the memory of my mother playing the koto. *I watched her play in her shadow through rice paper walls. I imagined her cradling the* koto *with eyes fixated on it while I reveled in the sweetness of her chords.* I beg, *let me be*, as war's brutal truth readies to intrude on my mind again.

> *The goal of the Japanese Empire was to achieve the East Asia Co-Prosperity Sphere under the philosophy that Asia should be ruled by Asians. The location of my final battle was the last line of defense against the Americans in retaking the Philippines. Part of me knew it was coming when our commanders circulated the news that General MacArthur said, "I shall return". No general would make such a public declaration without meaning it, I thought. Our superiors used this information to keep us alert to an oncoming onslaught. We heard the artillery hitting our defenses closer to the shores. Less than two months after MacArthur announced "I have returned" with confidence over the airwaves. My company and I retreated further into the jungle where we held our positions through the rainy season. It served as a crude introduction to the jungle. A wave of Americans and Filipinos found us, overran us. I fled.*

Since then, none of our planes with the *Hi no maru* on its sides and wings has flown over this valley.

Day 3

Rain pours. I dig. Water and mud avalanche back into the large trench with faceless bodies piled next to it. Other soldiers join and we pair-up to toss the bodies into their shared grave, each one splashing in the large pool of muddy water. The last body splashes in. We fill the trench with mud. The mound of mud washes flat and an inch of water covers the trench, which makes the imprint of the gravesite look like a pond.

An arm rises. "Kaiyo," a voice calls.

I stare at the arm that reaches towards me.

"Come on. Jump in," the voice continues, triggering my taphephobia. Shiro emerges from the pond. My fear is rinsed away. We jump in the pond with childlike joy, racing to the vine-filled bottom. Glancing at each other through the murky water to invoke a challenge, we race back to the top. I watch Shiro rise to the surface, but despite my attempt to swim up, I remain at the bottom with vines wrapped around my legs. My mother and father swim among the vines, and my wife Tamiko's blurred image looks down into the pond from the shore, waving for me to come up. I fight to free myself, panic, and hear the creaking of the old tree. The tree's shadow reaches me at the bottom of the pond. I reach for the shadow, and although I remain submerged, I no longer panic. The tree creaks louder in oneiric ambiguity.

I wake to wind gusting, leaves rattling, tree creaking in the dim glow of early morning, and to shadows of the old tree's branches swaying over me. Water plunks into the canteen. I release my clasp off a handful of soil, heart still racing, and skin hot. A large gathering of birds swoop and perch within a small group of trees and bushes. I'm drawn to inspect what lures the birds. *Do they pick at a carcass? Feed on fallen fruit? Perhaps it's a swarm of insects they feast on.* The birds scatter upon my approach in the morning shade of a waking sun. I clear through a circle of bushes and greet the reflective rolling water of a pond. *An oasis after all.*

I think of those innocent Filipinos caught in the crossfire as I kneel at the side of the pond staring at my reflection. *Ha. Who am I fooling? It was murder. It's cold-blooded murder, that's what it was.* Debris from the surrounding trees and bushes float on top of the pond. I reach down to scoop up water with one hand, examine it by holding the water in my cupped hand up to the available light, then smell it. I lick a single droplet running off my finger. Yesterday's rain satisfying my thirst makes it easier to toss the water aside. *Fire. I must boil the water.* If I don't build a fire or find another source of water soon, then I will be forced to drink the pond water as is.

I lie looking out the den for the first half of the day, with my ear resting on my hand atop the coolness of a shaded, moist ground. My eyes run up the trunk of the old tree, to the tangled branches. Stomach pangs press against my ribs. If my stomach could leap from my body in an independent search for food, it would. *Go for it. Find some food because I can't. You are more determined and courageous than me.*

I entertain the idea that surrender or capture would satisfy my hunger. *They are bound to feed me.* I've forgotten the taste of normal food. It isn't the shame of defeat or even death that I fear most anymore, it's the fear of facing cruel justice at the hands of those seeking vengeance. The thought of facing my accusers, the people I wronged, fills me, this murderer, with terror. I shift my thoughts to Tamiko and Maeko. *Can I face them again?*

Am I dead to them? With my predicament reframed, it doesn't seem too bad to be stuck here alone, nor to die from thirst or starvation.

I turn to the twig marker I placed in the ground yesterday and wait until the edge of the sun-streak is far past it. I put on my boots without socks and struggle to maintain balance trekking across the sandy soil. *Protein is what I need. Water and protein. Water and protein.* My boots sink into the soil, the blazing heat of the sun sapping more strength and the dust of burning sand clogging my nostrils. I reach the coconut tree and look up. *I can't climb this. Is there protein in coconut?* I kick the tree with the side of my foot in frustration, and with the small hope a coconut will drop. The tree, planted firmly in the soil, does not rattle. The act only adds to the soreness of my already scabbed, blistered feet.

"I'll get you," I say, looking up to the coconut.

The jungle floor surrounding the tree is spread with coconut fronds. There's a buzz. *Mosquito,* my eyes catching the source of the sound. I continue to search the ground for coconuts. Another buzz. I follow the sound but cannot find the mosquito. I'm back and forth between the den and the coconut tree, hiding from an imaginary plane and re-emerging, hiding, and re-emerging.

Later in the afternoon, another buzz. The buzz gets louder. I stop, listen. *A plane.* On hearing the rumble of a choking motor, much like the changing gears of a motorcycle, I plant one foot preparing to sprint off. *A coconut!* I marvel, spotting one under the low-lying branches of a bush. I snag it off the ground before rushing away, leaving behind the sway of branches that tried to hide the coconut from me and juggling it between two hands to prevent myself from dropping the nut-like fruit as I run. My pathway to the den is more precise this time, and I make it back before the plane passes overhead. *Reckless,* I think, knocking my left temple with the heel of my hand. What I thought would happen to that coconut, I couldn't say, except that I refused to lose it after getting so close. I stick another twig into the ground, marking the position of the sunlight coming through the cleft.

Holding the coconut up before me, I examine the fray of the dry husk, looking closely as though I'm bound to find out it's not really a coconut. *Maybe it's empty, hollow.* I jam my bayonet knife into the husk, and begin prying away at the fibrous membrane, thinking *what could I use the husk for? Sponge? String? Can I eat it? Tinder.* I yank the rest of the husk off with my hands, to reveal the round coconut shell, and toss the husk out in the open atop the hot sandy soil for it to dry further. The coconut shell is small, round like the candlepin bowling ball I encountered marching through the city of Balanga.

> *We lined the streets, marching in unison, while small bands of Japanese soldiers from another company maraud the villagers' belongings.*
> *"What is this?" a ransacking soldier asked the unsuspecting Filipino business owner.*
> *"A candlepin bowling bowl," the man answered.*
> *The soldier tossed the ball towards the street ahead of me as we marched, and it rolled into the roadside drainage canal. "It can be used as a weapon," he told the owner as other soldiers tossed out the remaining balls from the old community hall turned bowling alley. Men ahead of me picked up the balls and placed it in their knapsacks. I picked up one as I walked by but couldn't make sense of what I would use it for, or what the other soldiers planned to do with it. We kept marching and I handed it over my shoulder to the soldier behind me. Later, that same soldier used the ball as a weapon against an innocent Filipino man standing too*

close to the marching column as if he knew exactly what he'd be using it for when he took it from me. I was content to see this soldier die in battle weeks later.

I set the coconut aside and drag in a stone from outside the den, and flat enough to use as a small table. Cupping each end of the coconut with my hands, I raise it above my head, and strike the shell against one corner of the stone in a long downward motion suspecting it may just turn out to be one of those bowling balls and bounce right back into my face. Coconut water squirts out the cracks. *Not a bowling ball*. I cup the water in the bottom half and pull apart the two halves. *Not hollow,* after seeing the white flesh, then drink the coconut water. Using my knife to carve out chunks of clean, white coconut meat, I eat one large piece at a time as the pieces separate easily from the coconut shell as if they were pieces of white chocolate, melted then cooled to solidify in a wood bowl. I absorb the remaining bits with the tips of my wet fingers. The thought of eating the shell crosses my mind. *I would hate pooping that thing out.* The emptied, half-shell replaces the canteen under the dripping water. The wider radius of the shell catches more water from the array of imprecise drips as they plop onto the inside curvature, roll down, and collect in the middle. Although never climbing to retrieve the hanging coconut, I'm left with a sense of accomplishment. *Small step forward.*

The leaves rattle and branches sway in the afternoon breeze, breaking the monotony in the stillness and silence. The insects I pick at provide little to make up for the long absence of proper food. My stomach tries to speak to me through its growls.

"Calm down," I tell it.

"Grrrrr," it tells me.

Is it in pleasure or dismay?

In less than half an hour, it's clear the coconut has loosened my bowels and whatever liquid remains within me looks to escape. I step outside the den, walk over to a bush, and use my knife to dig a small hole into which I have no choice but allow my body to flush out much of my remaining liquids. *A big step backwards.* My stomach settles as the evening progresses.

"Rest now," I tell it.

My energy and mental acuteness take a dive, hurling me into delusion by the time night arrives. Tamiko and Maeko watching me from the darkness is the prelude to sleep, the white of their eyes appear and disappear in the blackness with each blink. What I do remember is that they have matching eyes, as if drawn on by the talented hands of a calligrapher in two separate soft curves for the top and bottom with the airbrushed brown of their pupils bleeding into the white of their cornea. It's hard to remember if I ever gave a proper look at them after returning from Manchuria.

I returned from basic training and exited the train in uniform. Shiro was there waiting. We embraced with big smiles on each of our faces. Shiro pushed me away with a smirk on his face.

"Looking important," he said, then laughed.

"When do you do your training?" I asked.

"Leaving at the end of the month," he told me.

"Enjoy your freedom while it lasts," I said, looking him directly in the eye. Shiro reached to help me with my knapsack. I jerked it away from him. "Just drive."

We hopped onto the motorcycle and Shiro jetted off, rushing to get me home to see Tamiko.

"You're going to kill me before I get to see Tamiko," I shouted into Shiro's ear, over the loud roar of the engine and wind. Shiro, skirting corners, turned back to me.

"She's been waiting long enough," he said.

Once on the long straight dirt road leading to Tamiko's family's home, I saw a single figure in the distance, standing in front of the house. Tamiko's figure grew on approach and the large, pregnant belly filled her dress. As we pulled up, her smile exposed the whites of her teeth, and then I saw the sparkle in her eyes.

"Welcome back, my love," she told me, kissing my cheek.

"Come here, my beautiful wife," I said, as I grabbed her by the waist, reeled her in for a hug, and kissed her.

"Calm down, mister," said Shiro, "save all the kissing for after I leave."

I kneeled on one knee and put my ear on Tamiko's belly, then rested my hand there.

"Papa's home," I spoke into her belly as if it was a large microphone. Tamiko flinched to a movement in her belly and pulled my hand away as if I had just touched a hot stove. We looked at each other with eyes wide.

"She heard you," Tamiko told me.

I turned to Shiro, "She responded to my voice."

We shared wide-eyed glances between us before I placed my hand on Tamiko's belly again.

"Can you hear me, my child?"

That night, my ear rested on Tamiko's belly. I sang the Japanese national anthem to Maeko.

"Seven days is not very long," said a wide-awake Tamiko after finding out I was off to Manchuria soon.

My dreary, relaxed eyes reopened, and I groaned in ac-

knowledgement.

"How do they expect soldiers to have a family if they're always away?"

"It's our duty, Tamiko," I responded.

She paused, then raised her voice in frustration, "For what?"

We remained silent for a minute.

"I've heard awful things about the Sino-Japanese war," she continued.

"Like what?"

"Bad things, violent things." "It's war, Tamiko."

"People die," she said, her voice pitching.

I removed my hand from Tamiko's belly and rubbed her leg.

"I'll be ok," I told her, before returning my hand to her belly after that empty promise.

On the morning of my departure, I hugged Tamiko long and tight. Shiro's motorcycle rumbled in the background.

"It'll be ok," I whispered to her.

"Come back for your daughter," she whispered back. I hopped on to the motorcycle, giving Tamiko one last glance and smile, as Shiro drove me off. Her figure shrunk in the distance until I couldn't see her anymore. I held that gaze as if she could still see me looking at her.

The convoy from Shanghai to Nanking was a long journey over roads which rattled every part of a soldier's body. The canvas walls of the lorry hid our eyes from the death that plagued the roadsides. Only through the flapping canvas, which would open and close between the loose ties hooked to the truck, could I glimpse the blood-stained ground. Some soldiers vomited from a combination of the bumpy ride and putrid smells. Not until arriving at Nanking and smelling the unfiltered, overwhelming stench of death, and seeing the battered corpses littering the city, did the rest of us heave up the rations we'd put into our bodies hours before.

I was one of the new soldiers deployed to Nanking to defend the city alongside many battle-hardened soldiers. Large groups of virgin soldiers were sent off to replenish the advancing Japanese front. I was assigned to a guard post within the heart of the city. This post was at the intersection of diverging roads suffocated by small buildings, horseless carts, and abandoned bamboo roadside markets stripped bare by my earlier comrades. Blasted fragments of brick, rock, bamboo, and wood debris littered the streets. Chinese civilians who chose not to flee became target practice when one occasionally sprinted from one building to another. Pop! And the Chinese civilian dropped fast to the ground as if their legs were swiped from under them. Until finally, on order of our superiors, innocent civilians walking the streets were no longer targets, contradicting the "Three Alls Policy" of kill all, loot all, burn all. As each day passed, more Chinese walked the streets and the daily lives of us Japanese soldiers normalized as if we were fellow citizens. The roadside bamboo markets restocked and reopened. We paid with items stolen from the houses and buildings of that same city. Some vendors received the exact same items stolen from them months earlier as payment.

"Restore order and a functioning society," our superiors told us. "This is your home for now."

But it was never peaceful. The execution of civilians, including children, suspected of conspiring against the Japanese was commonplace in the streets, and they were often filed out and shot in the open. I received Tamiko's letter the same week I witnessed the first group of executions. She wrote we were expecting a girl. Doubt over bringing a child into this world stood forefront in my mind. Would she one day be a victim like these executed kids, should Japan lose the war? Would I be there to protect her? In the week before we were to vacate Nanking, the Three Alls Policy came back into effect. "Leave behind nothing," we were told, "not even a rat burrowed deep in its hole."

The honor of appeasing the Empire of Japan, so they thought, allowed for the rationale of such acts. I started by avoiding precise aiming, hoping to give enough time for the victim to find cover on the missed shot only to find out it only delayed the inevitable and sometimes more gruesome death. The nightmares began that night after committing my first murders. I did everything I could to avoid killing another soul. It's nothing like the movies. A soldier in my unit had lost his mind from the guilt and eventually killed himself. The thought of doing the same crossed my mind but being there for my soon-to-be-born daughter kept me from doing so. The commanding officers seemed pleased that the soldier killed himself, seeing him as a liability.

All the while, I worried of Tamiko and Maeko's safety with their letters a hit or miss of finding me on the battlefield. Without much resistance in Manchuria, deployment there was a training ground for the real battles of the future which would have more powerful adversaries. I killed, was wounded by a stray bullet that passed through the edge of my torso, but I had yet to fight in a real battle. Killing someone that aims to kill me is a sign of a true soldier. Killing unarmed, innocent, civilians is cowardly, murder.

Our regiment was sent back to Japan after three, long, excruciating years, while other freshly trained soldiers replaced us. Tamiko and Maeko moved into a home, provided to us by her parents, on the other side of Hiroshima. I returned to Tamiko and baby Maeko preoccupied, numb, and without the capacity to connect with them. The faces of murdered women and children that I thought forgotten, return. My mind occupied by the horrors and emotions locked in an iron case to which no one holds the key.

I was there for Maeko's first day of preschool. Tamiko and I walked up the stairs to the entrance of Hiroto Elementary. Tamiko reached out to help Maeko up the stairs, but instead, Maeko reached out to grab my hand. It was the first sign of affection towards me, a stranger, an absent father, but the warmth of the moment couldn't penetrate my hardened exterior.

Day 4

Smoke floats over the dead bodies strewn across the field, separating the two entrenched opposing factions. The bodies lie in the sun all day, rotting in their faded uniforms. The stench lingers in the nighttime coolness as moonlight reflects off blades of grass and the liquefying skin of the dead soldiers. Dark figures wait on the other side as if they're a reflection of my comrades and me. The night sky sparkles. I reach forward, poke my finger towards the stars, and swirl my hand. The stars follow my swirling finger. The sky splashes and stars ripple, along with a blurry reflection of myself. Shiro, as a child, stands next to me with a big smile.

"We should go home, Kaiyo. It's late." I gaze up at the stars and point.

"But look at the stars, Shiro. They're so bright out here."

We both gaze up in silence together, before walking into the nighttime jungle.

"You go first," Shiro stops and looks towards me to lead the way.

I walk ahead of him. "This way," I say without looking back.

Shiro doesn't respond, and when I turn around, he's gone.

"Shiro?"

I retrace my steps. A soldier's dead body lies there on the path. As I get close, I recognize the face.

"Shiro!" I cry, kneeling next to his gunshot-ridden, sagging, bloodied body. I fixate on Shiro's eyes, and he's unable to look back through his dark, lifeless pupils. A rush of guilt fills me.

I wake in the middle of the night, alert and feeling empty, as if Shiro and our brotherly bond is severed. The tail of a glowing cloud of stardust is framed in the hexagonal shape of the cleft. I reset my sleeping position by crawling over to the den's entrance, sticking my head out, and lying down on my back, looking up to the full body of stardust floating among the blackness. Using what little I know about astronomy, I locate the Big Dipper and Little Dipper and point to the brightest star.

"North," I whisper.

I carve an arrow with my knife onto the surface above the entrance, pointing the arrow towards what I think is Japan. *Maeko. Tamiko. Shiro. I hope you have not given up on me.* I watch the stars sparkle long enough to follow their movement along the night sky before falling asleep.

I wake to the blue glow of early dawn. My body lies halfway out of the den, exposed from tossing and turning during sleep. I pop up and survey the area for any peering eyes, before crawling back under full cover of the den. The expectation of a passing plane keeps me in the den as the punishing heat of the sun bakes the jungle. The plane passes overhead. I peek out of the entrance to watch the plane dive into the valley, the glossy paint of its white star reflecting the sun onto my face like the flash of a camera. The drone fades. *Now's the time. Find food.* I exit, paying little mind to the lingering hum in the air. As I walk over to inspect the first group of trees and bushes, the drone returns. I walk back towards the den, then run when I realize the plane is coming around the ridge again. The den is too far. *In the bushes? Rush to bury myself in the leaves? Hold branches over my head? Idle up close against a tree? Decide!* I take five long running strides towards the pond and dive in headfirst at an angle, keeping my arms and legs tight against my body to limit the splash. Having never checked the depth of the pond, I prepare myself for impact. The water slows my momentum and I drift along the concave base of the pond, dragging my finger on the bottom. I look up through the undulating water to flip-flopping sunlight and treetops. The pond is shielded by a circle of trees and bushes, with a clearing directly above. I hide in a dark corner of the pond, shadowed by tall grass, keeping myself at the bottom by slowly releasing air from my lungs. The rippling waves have calmed to a sway. The blurred shape of the plane passes overhead.

One. Two. Three. I push off the bottom of the pond with my legs and shoot to the surface. I emerge, sucking in air as soon as I feel the water roll off my lips. *Close call.* Gunshots escalate in the valley. *Have they found me? Should I abandon the nook?* The battle carries on, the skirmish concentrated in one location. Relinquishing this spot would likely mean my demise at the hands of the jungle, if not by the enemy. I'll make my last stand here. *Is it courage when I have no choice but to face the enemy?*

I didn't get to see Maeko's face when I fled from my family, but imagined tears on her cheeks as she hid in her room. Tears of hurt and not tears because her father was leaving. Looking at Tamiko's face as I walked out of the door, I saw disappointment. Those final memories drown hope of ever redeeming myself. I didn't notice then the many glances Maeko gave me, as if to say, "Who is this man in our home?" But maybe she was simply looking to catch me glancing her way one time so she could tell her papa something, as little girls often do.

The sun retreats behind the ridge, the distant mountain range swallowing that unforgiving fireball. With dusk settled in, I exit the den, rake up dry leaves with my hands, and drop them in a line along the edge on this side of the barrier, expecting that the crunching of leaves will alert me of any approaching threats. I kneel at the triangle opening of the den, rifle in hand, eyes peering through the foliage, ears perked, and nose sifting the air for the soldiers' musk. *You will not take me alive.* I fall asleep on my knees, leaning against one side of the entrance, jolting myself awake to look around throughout the night, then going back to sleep. All I've come to love is at stake. An empire that's lost its way is not one of them.

Day 5

Dogs, as if rabid, tear shreds of meat hanging from a caribou carcass on the side of the road. They growl and snap at each other as we march into the village alongside a caravan of jeeps and trucks. Vultures peer down from their perches on surrounding trees. One dog turns and barks at us, displaying his fangs, oblivious to what little power he has over us. I march past the dog, staying in sync with the other soldiers and keeping my head facing forward, even though I sense the dog's urge to bite the back of my leg. He barks and growls at the soldiers behind me. Pop! A Squeal. Silence.

I hop onto a truck with some soldiers hanging on the sides. I find a seat on the opened gate at the rear. We rumble and squeak through the potholes. Looking down at my dangling feet, the potholes turn into carcasses of caribou and dogs that smell of fish. My body slides side to side, slamming against the cold steel of the truck's frame before the ride sways over shallow puddles.

Shiro and I sit at the rear of my father's caribou wagon. Our feet dangle. My father steers with a rope hooked to the caribou's nose, veering left around a large pothole. A heron, catching a free ride on the caribou's back, flaps its wings to keep balance, then returns to picking insects off the caribou's skin. Our feet are splashed with the muddy water of the puddles. Shiro taps my shoulder and points. I look down at my legs and feet, caked with layers of mud. We giggle.

"Hey!" my father shouts.

I become aware of my dream state, the vividness of it staying with me. My eyes crack open, but I continue to play out a version of my childhood and soon am back in my dream.

Shiro and I are careful to mute our giggles and cover our smiles. Another splash and our smiles return with pent-up

> *giggles. We pass a large pile of fish emanating a strong odor in the heat. I am haunted by the face of a young Filipina girl trapped in the pile, who keeps resurfacing in my dreams since finding the nook.*
> *"Save you," she calls out, reaching for me.*

I wake to the flutter, swoosh, and chirps of birds, and the smell of fish. I sniff the air and follow the scent to the pond. Lying there is a dead fish at the water's edge, swarmed by ants and with strings of white flesh hanging from its bones. *Who put the fish there?* I panic, scan the area for someone lurking, then look over to the pond.

I remove my clothes, jump in, and search within the murky water. I locate a group of tilapias.

"Fish," I say in excitement while submerged, choking on water that sneaks into my throat.

I try pinning the fish against the shore, but they skirt past me. I exit the pond, make a spear from a long stick by shaving one end into a point, jump into the water, and stab at the fish. The water is too deep and the fish too fast. *A net or basket may work. I have neither. My grenade?* I fight to keep a measured approach and move the fish carcass out into the open, closer to the den. *Bring me some food,* I implore, hoping the strong smell attracts those mysterious varmints always rustling through the leaves.

Today, the passing plane's thin and distorted shadow skims across the nook like a preying hawk. I firm up the outer two markers and remove the other twigs, relying on the earliest and latest as a cautious time frame. The dry leaves rustle around me. Those ghost-like varmints, perhaps aware of my trap, refuse to venture out to the fish carcass. *Varmints? Snakes?* Little do they know I have no method of catching them in the act of nibbling at the bait. *Chase them. Stomp them. Meat,* I think each time I hear them. The meat is lost if I shoot the small things. *Come on, you damn creatures. Show yourselves.*

I turn my attention to the less mysterious, and follow the movement of those swooping birds, trying to track the location of their nests. But when evening arrives, I lose sight of them in the dimmed light of dusk, never seeing where they retire to for the night. I think back to the tilapia. *Fish. Yeah, fish sounds perfect.* I sigh as the curtains close on today's performance of elusive fish, swooping birds, slithering snakes, and scurrying varmints. *Where are the monkeys?* Although we didn't often see monkeys close-up in warfare, the constant, far-off chatter signaled their presence. Their chatter did not contribute to this week's cacophony of sounds. I'm surrounded by food but cannot eat. The piercing pain in my stomach persists. *The apple. If I don't find food tomorrow, I'll eat it.*

Day 6

> *Villagers are lined up on the road in front of their homes. Two soldiers and I team up to inspect a hut because nobody stands in front to claim it. The window flaps and door are shut. I guard the front while the other two soldiers enter the hut with bayoneted rifles leading their way. The soldiers jam their bayonets into the wall of a small room at the rear before entering it. They rummage through the hut, pocketing a ring, a gold necklace with crucifix, a pair of reading glasses, and a small bottle of gin.*
>
> *Swiveling my head back and forth between guarding the entrance and watching the ransacking soldiers, I hear the rake of soil and bend down to peer into the dark underbelly*

of the hut. Between the log columns that lift the hut off the ground, I see a man, woman, and a young girl huddled together. They stare at me wide-eyed, frozen, and holding their breaths. I begin the motion to notify the soldiers above. I pause, then shoosh them by holding a finger to my lips. A rush of light shoots down on the family when the soldiers inside lift a hatch hidden under the rug. And in that flash of light, I find myself huddled with Tamiko and Maeko, looking up at the soldiers. The thrust of bayonets plunge into Tamiko and Maeko, but my arms are locked to my sides within the confined space. Their screams sear my ears; the helplessness boils my blood. The soldiers grin at me, "You failed," they tell me before their sharp blades plunge into my chest.

My eyes shoot open. I grab my chest, my heart thumping against my sternum and my body covered in sweat. Tamiko and Maeko's faces are clear in my thoughts, shame in my heart. *This nook is my refuge.*

Water. Food. Fire. I collect wood and the coconut husk laid out in the sun for the past three days. I place the dried coconut husk tinder in a hand-pressed concave within the sandy soil inside the den and pick the two driest sticks from the pile of collected wood. I rub the two sticks together. *Something like this,* I think, recalling my training. After about an hour, the action yields nothing except a sweatier, weaker, thirstier, and more hopeless self. *Fire. Water. Food.*

The tender overlay of the morning jungle eases my angst. Rat-a-tat-tat! The thunderous vibration of not-too-distant machine gun fire launches birds, hidden within the trees, from their perch and into the open air. I pop up, grab my rifle, and stand guard. Pop! Boom! Rat-a-tat-tat! The drone of planes joins the commotion. I study their sound. The scent of gunpowder reaches me. *This is it. They are coming for me. Full assault.* I visualize a group of men breaking through the barrier. *I will take out the leader.* I plan. I plot. *No! They will not come charging through. They will hide in the cover of the barrier and shoot at me from there. I'll be trapped inside the den.* I exit and position myself at the edge of the nook, at the front-cliff-wall, looking down for the approaching enemy. *The high ground. Maintain advantage of high ground.* Our battle training was much more thorough than our survival training. *I'll retreat to the den if needed. Fallback position. The two slabs will protect me from gunfire coming from the sides. The rock I cracked the coconut on is still there. I'll use that for cover. It's big enough. I'll make my last stand there, in the den. Bushido! Regain my honor.* I am a soldier again. My right hand trembles.

The booms stop, the planes fly away, then the rat-a-tat trickles to a stop. I return to the den and lie on my belly behind the rock with my rifle barrel resting on top, aimed at the barrier of foliage. *You won't catch me off guard.* My energy spent from a day on high-alert, a hint of who I was before the war returns to me in the lullaby of the nighttime stir. *Honor? Bushido?* The idea is now fickle, with my newfound independence. *I must survive.*

I daydream of home. *Tamiko, her touch. Maeko, her laughter. Shiro, our brotherhood. Food. Yakisoba topped with charred beef strips and the glaze of teriyaki sauce poured over.* Yes, food is what I think of now. This is what I really want. In fact, anything cooked. *Fire, Fire, Fire. I'll cook tilapia.* I drift off, nearly falling asleep. *A slither?* I shiver. *Snake!* I jump up and snag my rifle with the bayonet attached. I aim the blade before lifting the knapsack off the ground. *Nothing.* "Don't lose it, must hold on to my sanity," I tell myself, my tongue and throat aching with dryness. *Water. Fire. Food. Water. The apple! How can I forget? I must have planned this. Wait a little longer. Discipline.*

My eyes shutter open and close as thoughts of the apple fight with fatigue. I open my eyes, rise to my knees, stand the rifle next to the entrance, and remove the apple from the knapsack, my eyes fixated on it. *Discipline? I need to eat.* My chapped lip tears along the deepest wrinkle as I open wide to bite. The blood colors the apple flesh. I suck up the apple's juice, which escapes down the side of my mouth, then chew and swallow the apple flesh, finishing the tart fruit in two more large bites. I hold the stem, gnaw on it until soft, then swallow it before sucking the juices tucked away in the corners of my mouth. *My last meal?*

A flickering thought of reuniting with Tamiko and Maeko goes dark. *I'm dead to them anyway.* The camouflage of the jungle seduces me to die here, my will dried up in the drought of the most basic necessities. An empty shell of a man.

"You," Maeko would say, scolding me, her little finger pointing. "Mean man. You're not my papa."

I curl up and look into the jungle, which possesses everything needed, yet I welcome dying in solitude.

"Goodnight," I say, with little desire to wake the next morning.

Day 7

> *I stand guard, flinching to the gunshots. Dark figures appear in the jungle, move closer, then disappear. I lie against the foxhole wall and am soon surrounded by Filipino villagers.*
>
> *"Jap!" they shout, pointing down at me.*

A catholic priest in his white robe and purple sash parts the crowd and stands at the edge of the foxhole, looking down at me.

"Water?" he asks.

I nod. A villager gives the priest a bucket of water while the other villagers continue to shout.

"Kill the Jap!" "Don't help him."

"Murderer!"

I lick my lips. The priest tosses the water onto me, and I am unable to catch any with my opened mouth as it splashes over my forehead and wets my hair. The villagers stop shouting.

I look up, my eyes begging before my words. "More water please?"

"You're not ready," the priest replies.

The crowd is silent.

"You're free. You're free to go," he says before walking away.

The villagers follow the priest.

After everyone clears and I'm alone, an old woman wandering the jungle calls out, "Water."

I stick my head out of the foxhole, licking my dry lips.

"Where's my water?" she cries, begging for someone to help her.

I locate a bucket yards away and crawl out on my belly, grab the bucket, and pull it into the foxhole under cover of darkness.

"Water," the woman calls out again, walking past the foxhole. I press against the soil wall and remain silent. Her calls for water fade as she walks away. When I no longer hear her voice, I lift the bucket over my head and tilt it towards me to drink. The moonlight illuminates the inside of the bucket,

full of snakes. Before I can stop the momentum, the snakes slide onto my face.

I wake with both arms across my face, breathing heavily, and sapped of spirit. I have no desire to turn my head and look out of the entrance. My world has shrunk to the den. *Let my misery end here.* I haven't the strength, the wits, to carry on. If I survive, there will be no one to welcome me back. *Tamiko? No. Maeko? No.* Only Shiro, if he survived the war. The long-held vision of me dying peacefully on my family farm, lying in the same childhood bed, with the pink cherry blossoms floating onto the bedroom floor and their sweet scent putting me into a forever sleep, is only a fantasy.

There's a coolness in the air as fog rolls through the valley, easing the relentless heat. I close my eyes and sleep until the fog burns off, turning to my side when the heat nags. Now facing the entrance, dry and tired eyes half-closed, I see the blur of a green and brown blotched jungle in the background. I close my eyelids and pay no attention to whether a plane flies by today, resting until evening, void of sound, arrives. After the grand task of sitting up, I cross my legs and close my eyes.

"Ooooommm," I hum from deep within my diaphragm, grasping for inspiration and my sanity through meditation.

I open my eyes, looking and listening, as if answers await me. I close my eyes again and take a deep breath.

"Ooooommm," I hum on my exhale.

Sweet cords of the *koto* join the awakening nocturnal rhythms of my surroundings as a prelude to sleep.

"Play. Play for me," I say softly, my eyes looking over the landscape through the triangular exit of the den. *Kami.*

Year 1

Day 8

I struggle to open my eyes. *How long have I been asleep?* I lie, fetal and rejuvenated, without any lingering thoughts of my dreams. The last time I remember feeling this refreshed after a good night's sleep was when my parents went out of town for the weekend.

Shiro came over early Saturday morning, minutes after my parents left for the weekend to visit my Aunt Hotaru in Sapporo. I suspected that since the city was home to Japan's foremost brewery, it was extra incentive for my father to join my mother, and he flirted more with Aunt Hotaru than he did with my mother.

"What should we do today?" I asked Shiro, after he helped finish my daily chores. "The farm is ours for the next two days."

Shiro looked over to my father's rifle mounted on the wall.

> *"Target practice?"*
>
> *After a few seconds of me not replying, he looked to the white ceramic bottle of Bimbo Tokkuri sake.*
>
> *"I'm not going to abuse my freedom. I have limits," I interjected. "They may never leave me alone at the house again."*
>
> *Instead, Shiro and I invited over everyone we knew. The nine of us played a 4 vs 4 makeshift game of war using every corner of the property as hiding places, with me as the referee. I knew of all the hiding places and made the rules on my—at least for the weekend—land.*
>
> *That first night there alone, I laid there and wondered whether I should have shot cannikins off the tree stump at the edge of the property or tasted sake for the first time. My mind seesawed between the two. Gazing from the warmth of my bed, the moonlight accentuated the dark lines of the distant mountain range. Solitude and the short-lived autonomy drew me into a deep sleep unlike ever before.*

This is home, I think, hearing the familiar sounds and looking out to the familiar landscape from the warmth of the den. I look down to my wiry frame on the verge of emaciating. My beard is thickening but not yet thick enough to cover the scar across my cheek. I run my finger over the smooth surface of the scar where hair never grows. If someone didn't know me before the war, they might think I was in a fight with the enemy. And if that someone should ever ask, I would tell them something of the sort.

"What would you do if an enemy soldier charged at you ready to plunge his bayonet into your heart? You either take it in the heart or block the thrusting rifle and push it towards another part of your body."

A young boy would have the most interest in such a thing, and this theoretical boy follows up with, "You were in hand-to-hand combat with the enemy?" wide-eyed with intrigue, just as I was prone to be as a boy.

But whatever the follow up question, I would jump in before he could ask it.

"Kid," I would say in a scolding tone as the boy readies to roll the next word off his tongue, "stay away from war—any violence." Perhaps I would point my finger in his face. "It's not like what you read in books or see in movies."

Although sincere in my convictions about war, there is less shame in misleading someone than confessing it was self-inflicted after that night of my drunken rampage aimed at Tamiko and Maeko.

I look up to the peak. *Imagine what I can see from there. The enemy, a river, a village. I would command this area from there.*

The day will come. Yet, I find myself confined to the den without food or enough clean water. *Fire. How?* I spend the morning thinking of just that and if I should even try. *How? How? How? And the smoke? It could give away my position.*

I curl up for the day, knowing that the enemy hunts for me and any of my comrades. *What next?* Some enemy hunt for revenge. Capture could mean a brutal death. *Is it true that time heals?*

"I need time," I say to myself while looking out to the jungle.

Maybe if I wait long enough, Tamiko and Maeko will forget the past, too, and give me another chance.

My rhythm with this environment is out of sync: my uniform and what it stands for, the cold hard steel of my rifle, even my movements and rugged ways are in vulgar contrast. My soul reeks of the wretched impurities. The adjoining standing monuments of rock slabs making up the den give me flashes of a place where my body decays as my final resting place. These pillars of stone are sepulchral-like, signifying my vast failures in life. *Rightly so,* I think.

"I need water," I say, digging deep into my soul and using the faint hope of reuniting with Tamiko and Maeko as motivation.

"Think, concentrate," pressing my palms against my temples as though I can squeeze out an idea for my next move.

Pop! Pop! Pop! The plague of war persists.

At dusk, the scout plane passes. I've come to realize keeping track of flight times are useless. A pilot is a soldier of the sky, after all, and making his flights unpredictable gives him the advantage. *Another failure. Failure of the mind.*

I build a small firepit in the center of the den with a ring of stones, then add to my stockpile of twigs, dry grass, leaves, and wood. *A lot of work if I can't ever start a fire,* I think. I take a large piece of wood, carve out a divot and a stick to fit into the divot, and spend the day waiting for the plane to pass. The plane passes overhead when the sun is at its highest point. I place the tip of the carved stick into the divot and roll the top half between my opened hands, using the sunlight coming through the cleft to further heat the point of friction. I rub until my hands are bright red and near drawing blood as I drip sweat, far from producing enough heat to create a spark. I resign to lying down and taking a break.

If this should be my final resting place as an isolato, my foggy mind is ready to surrender to it, but there's a sense of incompleteness that resists my surrender. Images of Tamiko and Maeko flash into my blank stare. The rhythm of the jungle plays in the background: a chirp here, a buzz there, and the breeze rattling the leaves—all within their own metered pace.

At nightfall, my eyes draw heavy, jaws loosen, and the beat of my heart slows. I crawl over to drink from the coconut cup by pouring it into the pocket of my lower lip, the most assured way to avoid ripping my chapped lips. Using my finger to collect the oily sheath from the side of my nose, I rub it onto my lips to soothe the dryness. I pick at ants that crawl around me without much thought, until the squish in my chewing reminds me of their mucus-like insides. *I must find some real meat.*

Day 9

My eyes shoot open.

"I am samurai," I say, popping up to my knees with the day's goal

clear.

I venture further out to the edge of the nook and stand near the cliff wall that drops into the valley. A foulness of rotting flesh reaches me in the push of air coming up from the valley. Walking along the edge of the cliff while sniffing the air, I follow the scent to the decomposing body of an American soldier. His body is propped up against the front-cliff-wall behind a group of bushes, as though the soldier found a final resting spot months before I arrived. The wall was a last obstacle he could not overcome before reaching the safety of the nook. *Not tough enough,* is my initial thought, as I pull my sleeve down to hide the subtle tremble in my right hand.

I climb down and cover my nose from an odor one never gets used to. He has no shoes, no shirt, and makeshift shorts from an old uniform held up by the fraying bamboo string he wears for a belt. Maggots, beetles, and ants are busy in and around his body. On his chest, close to his heart, rests a Bible with both hands draped over it, and spectacles are hooked onto his stiffened fingers. Propped up against a rock is a bolo with USAFFE carved onto the grip. I examine it by flipping it to both sides and running my finger along the blade, gauging the sharpness before sliding it between my thousand-stitch waistband. I look around for anyone who watches before checking his pockets, finding they are worn through with holes. I pry his hands away from the Bible. Moisture from his rotting flesh has seeped into the leather cover, staining the first few pages. The Bible opens to a creased page where the man's soiled fingers left behind streaks. I read, "And above all is love, which binds everything together in perfect harmony," standing out from the page before closing the Bible.

"The essence of the Bible is love and forgiveness," my Japanese American friend Curtis told me.

> *Curtis was born in San Francisco, as were his parents, and their parents too. He was twenty-one and lived in Japan for two years after graduating with a degree in literature and a minor in psychology from Berkeley. Because of him, what I learned about Christianity has intermixed with my pre-existing spiritual influences of Shintoism and Buddhism. Curtis inspired me to go to college. I started at the University of Hiroshima, but could not afford to finish. "Trying to understand the other part of me, my ancestors, the place and history that shaped the trajectory of my family," he said. He was learning Japanese while in Japan, but we went back and forth between English and Japanese when talking. He already knew some Japanese and I knew some English. I spoke in English, trying to improve my language skills, and he spoke in Japanese, trying to improve his. We helped one*

another, but it became a back-and-forth game of who's improving more.

Before leaving for America, he said he'll be in touch. I never received the letter he promised, so I sent a letter to him a year later. I figured he joined the military since he spoke of doing so during our time together, to prove his loyalty to America. If he had, he would be what's called a Nisei. Odd to think if he joined the army, how we could have fought in the same place against each other without ever knowing it. The only dividing force is our allegiance.

I place the Bible and spectacles aside, freeing my hands to toss leaves and branches on top of the soldier. The American's failure is to my benefit. If I had found him alive when I first emerged through the barrier and into the nook, we would have been in a standoff. My rifle versus his bolo. Perhaps a duel of bayonet versus bolo, because a gunshot would have tipped-off my pursuers. His failure to climb that wall could mean my survival through all of this. The morning is bright. I hurry back to the den with the bolo, spectacles, and Bible.

I test the grip of the bolo by chopping through the air, striking across my body once from the right, then switching hands and striking once from the left. I put on the spectacles after wiping the lenses clean, growing dizzy with my altered vision. I snap them off to avoid falling from a lost equilibrium. I sway, and my eyes shutter as I regain balance. Caressing the lines of the engraved writing on the Bible's leather cover, my fingers run along the H, the O, the L, the Y, then drop down, reversing direction along the E, the L, the B, the I, the B. *Nice craftsmanship.* I place the Bible next to the bolo, spectacles, and my knapsack.

Half the day passes with my mind jumping in my idleness to and from war, Tamiko, Maeko, Manchuria, death, destruction, Shiro, my parents, the farm, my final battle here, Tetsu, Hansuke, and different variations of order that sometimes come in flashes and other times in patient reverie. I pull out a bullet from the knapsack, pop off the rear of the bullet casing using the edge of my knife, dump out half of the gunpowder into the divot, and place a small pile of the dried threads of coconut husk over it. I then pop out one of the lenses from the spectacle's frame, place it in sunlight coming through the cleft, and angle the magnified light onto the pile of tinder and gunpowder. I keep the white dot of the magnified sunlight steady. *Do I even need the gunpowder for this?* A string of smoke rises, and seconds later, the gunpowder pops and sparks in a bombastic opening act to the flame. I place dry leaves on the flame. The popping gunpowder projects away some of the dry leaves like a grenade does to soldiers. I add more leaves, twigs, and branches. The fire grows large. I top the pile off with a log that releases pieces of burning leaves swirling into the air. A cloud of smoke filling the top half of the den seeps out of the cleft, though it disperses before rising above the canopy of trees. *Water.* I lie under the cloud of smoke and pop out a thin metal piece on the bottom of my canteen to remove a photo of Tamiko and Maeko. I place the photo between the pages of the Bible.

"You'll be safe there," I say, before placing the Bible on the small rock I used to crack open the coconut.

I crawl out of the den, fill my canteen with pond water accompanied by the debris on the surface, return to the den, and place the canteen on the crackling fire. When the water boils over and steam blows out of the top like the smokestack of a locomotive, I use my socks as gloves, remove the canteen from the fire, and drop it on one side of the firepit, the heat stinging my hands through the worn-thin socks. I stick my hand deep into the sand until I feel the soothing coolness.

Once the water cools, I drink, pausing to spit out a piece of wood and catch my breath. I sip, spitting out slivers of wood each time, then return to the pond once the canteen is empty. *Learn from my mistakes,* I tell myself. I place the cloth of my shirt over the canteen's opening as I submerge it into the pond to refill. The fabric filters the debris floating on the pond's surface from entering the canteen. I boil the water, drink it, then do it all over again to save a batch for later. I set the canteen aside for the night and snuff out the fire, leaving only a pile of red, hot embers. I scoop up the embers and enclose them in the coconut shells which have dried over the fire, set it at the edge of the firepit, and further insulate it by covering it with the warm soil and ashes from the pit.

The transition from afternoon to dusk yields a temporary pause in nature's stir, the chirp of an eager cricket the sole instrument. Darkness falls, masking my plight as I lose clear sight of what surrounds me until the mysterious nocturnal sounds and popping gunfire remind me where I am. I lie down with the fog of my hydrated mind lifted, even though my stomach still begs, and my body is lethargic. Thoughts of the dead American lying nearby cause me to toss and turn. *Who is this man? Does he have a family that still waits for him?*

Day 10

"I am not the enemy," a voice says.

I wake. It's morning. I put on my boots and return to the dead American soldier. *American Joe is what I'll call him. Joe,* I think, on approach.

"Hi there, Joe," I say. The whites of his eyes show through a gap in the layer of debris.

I clear the branches and leaves from his body, then dig a pit about three feet deep, three feet wide, and six feet tall, using the coconut shell and my hands on the soft-soiled downward slope a few yards away from the front-cliff-wall. I roll his body onto the layer of removed branches and drag Joe's corpse to the pit, leaving behind a trail of maggots. I roll Joe into his grave, the flail of his limbs swaying to one side, as if he's reaching for someone.

"Rest well, Joe," I say, before covering him with soil.

I place a large stone on top. Standing up stiff and straight, I salute. "My enemy you may be, but I respect you," I say, relaxing my stance.

Walking back up the slope, I avoid the trail of human flesh-eating, squirming maggots that would otherwise make good fish bait.

Fish? Coconut? Insects? I cycle through the options with a clearer mind from rehydration. The amount of energy it takes to climb the tree for one coconut is illogical. The amount of energy devising a fishing method, implementing it, and waiting without guarantee that I will catch anything, is also illogical. *Insects it is*. It takes less energy to collect the many insects which fly past my face and crawl at my feet. And now having the fire to cook them should make eating them more tolerable. I use a thin stick as a *kushi* and skewer the beetles over the fire like it was *yakitori*. The guts that didn't seep out during cooking squirt in my mouth, tasting much like nuts and shrimp. *For the sake of survival*, I tell myself as I eat.

Day 16

I've used up two more bullets because the embers don't always keep through the night when the air is cooler and moist. At this rate, I'll use all my bullets without taking a single shot for hunting. *What a waste.* I return to the coconut tree, searching for more fallen coconuts. *Where are the rest of the coconuts?* It's unlikely the tree only produced two—the one I picked up off the ground and the one that still hangs. I target the hanging coconut with small rocks, striking it with two consecutive throws. My baseball coach, Mr. Suzuki, is to be thanked for that.

> *I played center field. Although I experimented with every position, like most of us during the first month, center field was perfect for me. Far away from the action and room to roam.*
>
> *"Have confidence. Follow through," he told us during our first week of practice.*
>
> *"Teamwork. All about teamwork. Trust the guy next to you," Mr. Suzuki repeated during each practice, which prepared me for the army.*
>
> *Comparatively, Captain Mori would say, "The guy next to you can mean the difference between life and death. Just do your job. Don't forget your training."*
>
> *Shin played left field, Nobu played right. Shiro didn't play, because it conflicted with his judo classes. I would join him in judo practice when I didn't have baseball practice, and was encouraged by my ability to throw Shiro when sparring, despite him knowing many more of the judo moves. I perfected the* ippon seoi nage *and would throw him at least once per practice until he began competing in tournaments the following year. We each had our strengths—his, quickness and endurance; mine, balance and strength. I'd tell him I was also smarter, and he'd respond by telling me he's better looking.*

I hope you're ok, my brother.

The coconut hangs firm. Using a rock the size of a baseball, I cock my arm and throw it up, following through on my release as fingers shoot forward, pointing right at the coconut. The rock, much heavier than a baseball, falls short. I hop onto the tree, hug it, and shimmy my way a several feet up before hopping back off. My arms and legs are red, much like a sunburn topped with the white, flaking skin of scratches. Looking up to the coconut and calculating my options, I pick up the longest stick I can find and throw it at the coconut as if it is a spear. The stick, too long and lanky, bounces off the side of the tree and reverberates all the way down to the ground, then vibrates as if a toy with batteries was left on. *Useless,* I think, discouraged that a single tree remains a puzzle. *There are so many more puzzles to solve if I am to survive.* Looking down to the coconut fronds at my feet, I collect and spread them out on the den floor. They will keep the sandy soil from finding its way into my body's crevasses, and to act as a buffer from the ground's coldness during the night. *Small step forward.*

Weeks Later

Flies harass me, landing on my face and crawling over my emerging beard. My odor has lured flies away from my toilet along the rear-rock-wall near the den. I bathe at the pond and brush my teeth with the residue of charred wood, using my finger. Spreading a fresh set of coconut fronds for my mattress, I languish naked on their wax-like surface.

I start a fire soon before dusk, the fading light helping to hide the smoke, but not so dark as to give away the glow of flames. Water boiled, I exit the den, plunge my fingers into the decomposing leaves under the large tree, and flip over the tightly compact layer as if it were a stack of damp *washi* paper. Beetles, black ants, and centipedes flee for cover. Worms wriggle on the surface, the veins of their exposed burrow-tubes like a piece of abstract art made in the soil. I drop to one knee to collect beetles and place them in the clench of my other hand. I roast them on a *kushi*, waiting until their insides finish sizzling and oozing out. They cool. I eat. They're crunchier than last time, and the nutty shrimp flavor is milder.

"Hai," I say to the improvement.

It's nearly dusk and the fire crackles. *Is that a drone?* I listen. *Plane! The fire!* I douse the fire with water from the canteen.

I toss the sandy soil of the den on top of the fire, then place coconut fronds over that before throwing my moist shirt and pants on top of the coconut fronds permeating smoke. *Close call,* I think, freezing with my ear turned towards the sky, fixed on the drone until it is silent. "Don't come back, don't come back," I whisper to myself. *Let me be.*

I take my fingers, blackened from the charred wood, and rub them along the flat surface of the den's rock slab wall. I wipe off the smudged finger markings with my palm and pick up a half-burnt stick from the firepit. Pressing and twisting the pointed end against the wall, I mark the wall with a black dot. After six dots, I draw a circle around the dots and repeat three times. *21? For the person that finds my dead body someday.*

I revert to my childhood adventures, searching within that encyclopedia of experiences for solutions to my plight. Thoughts of my neighbor, Mrs. Tanaka, surface while sifting through my memories for useful information.

> *It was a crisp, cool, sunny day. A blue-sky background showed between the gaps in the branches of a Sato Nishiki cherry tree as we looked up. Shiro and I watched Mrs. Tanaka pick cherries with a long pole of bamboo sticks tied together, a rake the size of my hand on one end to yank the cherries off their stem, and a basket of equal proportion*

underneath the rake. I waited for Mrs. Tanaka to hand one of us the cherry picker as we sat, awed, when a group of cherries popped off their stem and fell into the basket.

"Can we try?" I asked when she finally glanced over our way. She handed the cherry picker to Shiro.

I should have asked, "Can I try?"

Shiro plucked one bunch, then handed the cherry picker to me. I plucked around thirty cherries before the outreach of an arm summoned the return of the cherry picker to her.

It could work, replacing the imagery of cherries with the coconut hanging from the tree. *But no bamboo.* I peel thin strips of bark from a tree and use them to tie together a series of branches to make a pole long enough to reach the coconut, with the thickest branch at the bottom, and the thinnest, lightest branch at the top. The pole is heavy and lopsided from the curves and unbalanced weight. The contraption reaches the coconut, and I use the pronged ends of two young, sprouting branches to rake over the stem of the coconut. I yank. The prongs snap, and the sudden jolt loosens the linked junctures before the pole collapses.

No clear evidence of my workmanship remains from the sprawled-out, broken pieces. The branches and strips of bark used as ties blend into the ground's debris onto which they've fallen. *Not a complete failure,* I think, as the coconut dangles looser. I toss a rock and it bounces off the coconut. I flip another rock in my hand like I'm warming up for a pitch. The coconut sways. I cock my arm. Before I can throw again, the coconut snaps off and thuds when it hits the ground, locking into its own imprint in the sandy soil. *Victory.*

I look to the sky. "Finally," I say, with my arms outstretched, when I meant to say, "Thank you."

Feasting on half the coconut, I savor every bit of one half and save the second half for tomorrow. By spacing out consumption of the two halves, the natural laxative loosens my bowels but doesn't flush me out like before. *I'm learning*.

***

It's early morning, and I wait until there's enough light to search for food but still enough darkness to conceal me. I scavenge, stopping beside the familiarity of a green, leafy, weed-like plant. I pull tight on the roots, then dig the topsoil off with the other hand, and pull. I dig. I pull. A tug-of-war with the ground ensues. In a burst of energy, I yank out a group of sweet potatoes from the compacted weight of the soil. The purplish hue of their leaves and the dangling, rattan-like roots are now visible.

"Ah yes, *kamotes*," as the Filipinos call them.

This word stands out among the other words in Tagalog.

> *A young man approached.*
> "Kamote, *po?" he asked, offering food, as the Filipinos tended to do, despite our hostile presence.*
> *I stared at him, trying to understand the words.*
> "Kamotes, *po?" he asked again, raising the sweet potato closer to my face.*
> *My attention turned to the cloth underneath the* kamote. *That, combined with the fact the man's face wasn't familiar to me, made me think the cloth was protecting the man from poisoning himself with the synthetic urethane it was dipped*

in.

One of the more social kids approached us. "Kuya?" *he asked the man, sensing our impasse.*

The man spoke to the boy in Tagalog. I picked up the word "kamain," *which means eat, and* "mainit," *for which I didn't know the translation. "You eat while it's still hot," the boy said to me in English.*

English is part of the regular curriculum in all the schools here. The man who offered the kamotes *likely never attended school.*

"It's a sweet potato," the boy told me. "Masarap."

I nodded to the man and eyed the boy, who watched me with an honest grin as I took the kamote *back to my comrades.*

We sliced the kamote *in half. Steam rose from the center, and we shared by scooping out the soft flesh with our fingers.*

When I looked back up, the boy wasn't in the spot where he handed me the kamote, *but I knew he watched from somewhere to see the enjoyment on our faces. It was more delicious on that day than what we call the* yamaimo *in Japan.*

I rest on my back, hands still gripping the *kamotes*, which lie across my belly as they rise and fall with my deep breathing. My body runs on fumes, and the starchiness of the potatoes will complement the diet of ants and beetles. If it wasn't rice, my mother would feed me *yamaimo*. To this day, I cannot understand why we were ever out of rice when we lived on a rice paddy. It happened several times. I do know my father wasn't very good with money, and rice was our currency. I guess I do know why, or probably why—geishas and gambling. But I'll give my father the benefit of the doubt and say it was those seasons of bad harvests that were often the culprit.

After catching my breath and when the sunlight leaks over the horizon into the valley, I wash the soiled *kamotes* in the pond, exposing the purple tint of their skin. The *kamotes*, hanging as I grip their roots, drip water onto my legs and feet as I walk back to the den. I place a *kamote* on the rock table, and slice it into six pieces with my knife. The hard flesh crunches like an apple and the fibrous texture of raw *kamote* is bland, though milkier than cooked *kamote*. I eat up this one *kamote* piece by piece throughout the day. It satisfies my taste buds and fills my shrunken belly. It does not suppress my deep craving for meat. *Fish.*

***

For the first time since providing Joe with a gravesite, I climb down the front-cliff-wall and walk towards the valley to find a pile of mangoes. *Fifth Column Spies*, I think, as the mangoes appear purposefully placed for me. These spies were Filipinos working with us Japanese. Maybe they somehow know I roam these parts. I put my rifle strap over my shoulder, gather as many mangoes as possible, holding them against my body, and walk back towards the nook. Rat-a-tat! I drop to the ground, letting go of the mangoes in the process. They roll away. I remove the rifle from my shoulder while on my belly. Rat-a-tat, rat-a-tat-tat, tat-tat, the vibrations rattle the trees and bushes as if they shiver from the threat. I clench the rifle.

"Shoot him," says a man with a Filipino accent.

A group of men rampage through the jungle perpendicular to me.
"Shoot the Jap," an American says.

Should I run? No. Stay still.

I take a deep breath, hold, and exhale like I did when blowing gently on Tamiko's neck before Manchuria. It is a ragtag group of Filipino and American men. The men, still wearing their makeshift uniforms as though they are a badge of honor, are USAFFE. *Your friends, Joe.* The United States Armed Forces Far East are part of the resistance movement of American soldiers who escaped to the jungle after Japanese occupation. A bitter and efficient group I must avoid, but a welcome alternative to the Huks, who are Filipino communists that joined the fight against the Japanese and are known for their swaying loyalties and extreme brutality. I sink behind the bushes.

Stay.

The men pass as I'm ready to release a load of air too large for my lungs.

Stay.

The men stop, turning back towards me.

Stay.

"This way," a man says.

My eyes shift with an expectation they'll spot me at any moment.

Hold it. Hold.

The crunch of their footsteps and their voices gain distance. I exhale.

I jump to my knees and scoop up three of the dropped mangoes before running away. Stumbling, I drop one and keep running. I cut left, then cut right, veering away from the voices now coming from different directions. If there's a group of idle soldiers, then I may find myself bowling right over them. I sprint through the jungle, avoiding entanglement within the bushes and vines as I twist, turn, and slide through the gaps. Ahead, a body hangs.

Comrade, I think, once I'm close enough to see the red patches on his uniform.

He's riddled with gunshots in a cruel game of target practice. It's a scene I wish to avoid, but keeping my direction, I run towards him. He is tall. *It's not Tetsu*. I look away, fearing my reaction to the lifeless face of Hansuke. I force myself to look up, my heart dropping into my stomach as I pass in the moment of *this could be Hansuke*. I decipher the blood-smeared, pale face. *It's not Hansuke.* If Tetsu or Hansuke were killed, I hope their deaths were quick. The soldier's eyes seem to follow me as I run past. This sends a chill through my body. *He's dead*, I tell myself, and hustle towards my peak showing itself high in the distance. Continuing my sprint and not stopping to catch my breath, I arrive at Joe's grave and drop the mangoes. Using the stone I placed on top of his grave as cover, I aim my rifle into the valley and watch for any of those fanned-out soldiers trailing behind the lead group. Rat-a-tat-tat. The soldiers circle back this way.

"Banzai!" a fellow Japanese soldier screams.

Tetsu?

I clench my rifle tight. *Bushido!* Looking to the grave.

I will die with honor.

I rise to one knee, heart beating fast while I map my charging path into the valley to join my comrade.

I'm not the enemy, I think, remembering that voice.

Bushido?

Honor and doubt pitted against each other, creating enough idleness to blunt the warrior in me.

Minutes later. Pop, pop, rat-a-tat-tat, pop. Silence. I lie back down

on my belly. *Tetsu. If that was you, I'm sorry, comrade. You are safe and at peace now.* The soldiers below trample through the valley, hidden under the cover of trees. *I'll wait it out.* Thoughts of Tetsu flood my mind. *The Japanese Empire won't remember him. His family will. I will remember you, Tetsu. My comrade.*

"It's just you and I," whispering to Joe.

It's near dusk when the swoosh and snapping of branches stop. I climb up the wall onto the platform of the nook and through the curtain of foliage, elated to be concealed again behind the natural barrier. Once inside the den, I drop myself onto the coconut frond floor. *Safe.*

I hunker down within the den, haunted by the face of the dead comrade and the scream of Tetsu. *It wasn't Tetsu*, I tell myself, to ease any guilt. I won't start a fire to boil water for at least three days. The enemy still looks to weed out every last one of us. *We are prey*. A snap of a branch. Someone lurks in the valley. Every one of my cautious movements, my hands trembling, is with the well-trained Filipino scout in my mind's forefront, as the regular soldier has resigned for the day. Broken branches and footprints are telegraphs to the scout, but the tread of my boots is worn flat, and his many comrades trampling nearby will create confusion.

The moonlight paints dark, mysterious, ominous silhouettes around and beyond.

I returned to the farm earlier than usual and sat under our tree on the grass-filled island in the center of the rice field, where the connected raised pathways dividing sections of the rice paddies met. The tree shadowed me in the remaining light of dusk, and a lantern flickered inside our house. Shadows stretched and shrank with movement from within. Hard-edged silhouettes appeared through the thin rice paper doors, but my father was out drinking with friends. The shadows danced within the house, drawing close, then apart. I heard my mother's voice but not her words, joined by the deep rumble of a man's voice. The two shadows crisscrossed several times. The door slid open as the man prepared to leave. A few soft words were exchanged before he exited. I squinted, thinking it would somehow give me a better vision through the darkness, but didn't recognize the man's tall, slender frame. The man walked away across the field at the rear of the house, and I watched him disappear into the darkness, the direction of his departure giving no additional clues. I stayed there under the tree, waiting for my father's return to detract attention from my own. My father's motorcycle rumbled down the pathway otherwise used for walking. When I entered the house, a flowery scent was in the air, casting suspicion onto them both. They each attempted to interact through the awkwardness of the perfume's scent. I slipped into my room and listened, hoping to catch clues as to who was guilty, by their tone and chosen words. No one spoke.

I avoided returning to the house unexpectedly thereafter when my father was away, and never saw the strange man around again. Prior to this night, my parents had taken me to the Shinto shrines and Buddhist temples as a young boy.

I wandered, touched what I wasn't supposed to, and talked when I shouldn't have. At the shrine, my parents washed their hands and mouths with water from the temizuya *before making an offering of money, ringing the bell, praying, and then clapping twice before bowing as we departed. At the temple, they would chant. I saw the shrine as a playground and the temple as a museum, the meaning of them not reaching me until I was old enough to read. Working on the farm and worship were the only things we did as a family. We rarely spoke on those occasions, unless necessary. It was not long after stumbling onto the strange man at our house with my mother, when even worship couldn't bring us together.*

Months Later

After failing to catch the tilapia with my hands several times over the months, I stand above the pond with one end of a long stick carved into a spear. I drive the spear into the water at the sight of their dark shapes blurred by the murky depths. I wait, locate, then thrust the spear again and again. It becomes like a child's game of stick-torpedo. *Maybe if I enter their world, I'll have a chance.* I jump into the pond, follow the tilapia, and try spearing them while underwater. Lazier with each attempt, I go through the motions, and my focus is pulled towards other solutions. *A multi-pronged spear? A net? Drain the pond?* I give myself one final push and thrust the spear with more vigor. The spear snaps. I exit the pond.

"Darn fish," I say, tossing the broken spear aside, the water dripping off me as I stand inglorious.

Give me protein. I walk fast back to the den like a pouting child and grab the grenade. Straddling the edge of the pond, eyes peering into the murky water, I pull the pin from the grenade, toss it in, and run to shield myself behind a tree. The muffled explosion fills the air. Water and debris rain down. I come out from behind the tree to find the pond near emptied of water and two dead tilapias floating in what remains. I take a savage-like bite of the exposed, raw, stringy white meat. I start a fire and spread open the fish by slicing down their middle, tossing the guts aside, and cooking them until light brown. I supplement my meal with the starchiness from half a *kamote* to dilute some of the protein. *Finally. Proper food. Meat.* My energy boosted but stomach unsettled, I resist eating more fish for at least four hours to avoid a protein-induced, rancid stomach.

It was a half day's trip to Kaita Bay, where my father was a weekend fisherman along with his fisherman friend, Minato. It seemed so easy to fish back then, with those large nets we cast overboard. At the age of five, and after our first day out on the boat together, my father and I walked from the dock to our wagon with two pails of fish. Geisha houses lined the streets at Horikawamachi. The thin bamboo string of the wood pail cut into my hand as I stumbled trying to keep the bucket, nearly as tall as me from bucket bottom to the stretched-out string handle, from dragging on the ground. I was proud to show anyone impressed with our day's catch while struggling to carry.

"Very good," an old man said, looking down into the pail, then smiling at me as if he should help. I continued lugging the pail down the street, trailing far behind my father.

A woman, face painted white and wearing a black kimono, walked out onto the first-floor balcony. The kimono was de-

signed with gold-colored crashing waves on the bottom half. I saw her before she saw me. Although I didn't understand the role of a geisha until years later, I knew the woman was a real-life representation of the gold-leaf artwork that hung in the sitting room of Shiro's home. She looked at me and smiled. I smiled back, lifting the bucket higher. Other geishas looked my way but never smiled at me like she did. It wasn't until I was ten years old when I learned the primary motivation behind a geisha's smile. Each year between the first smile and realizing this, I looked up to that first-floor balcony every time I walked down that street and smiled whenever I saw her.

***

I wake to monkeys calling in the distance. Stepping out of the den, I stretch and look to an unusual gamboge glow in the sky to the distant north. The glow is concentrated, taking up a small piece of the horizon's otherwise gray and white spectrum with the blue revealed in the sparse gaps of a cloud-filled sky. The clouds press against the atmospheric limits among the contrasting glow. It is like a child's artwork of cotton and orange and yellow paint. The raucous monkeys allow me to gauge their location at an adjoining mountain north of me. Playful or frantic, they abandon any discretion to their location. *Monkey meat. I hear it's delectable.* If I am to hunt them down, now is a good time. As I watch the glow fade, I work hard to decipher this phenomenon, attributing it to an unusual placement of cloud within the morning sunlight. The now uniform spectrum of dull gray and white horizon aligns with the monkeys' calmness. I lose them in their silence. *No monkey meat today.*

***

Months later and further away this time, the frantic monkeys wake me again. I look north to see a similar bright orange glow. The glow is more prominent and further east than previously. *Monkey meat!* I grab my rifle and track the monkeys' location, but before I can reach them, the glow fades out. They calm. Unable to track them, I imitate their howls. No response. I try again and imagine their heads tilting to this unusual noise.

"What weird animal is that?" the monkeys would say, if they could talk.

My calls persuade them to migrate to this mountain. I walk towards them. I stop and call again. They respond. I smile. But as I get closer and continue to call out, they migrate further into the jungle, moving away from my calls, as if the slight change in tone from excitement to desperation altered the meaning of my calls from "hello" to "monkey meat." I call out again. No response. Climbing up the side of the mountain, I locate the swaying treetops as they gain distance in a seamless transition from tree to tree. *No monkey meat today.*

The Rain

After months of torrential rain, the need to stretch my legs and arms swells over me, and I endure the sting of rain that blows hard against my skin, whipped by the roaring wind. There's more water than I know what to do with when it was scarce not long ago.

"Yes!" I shout, arms spread like wings and face looking upwards. "Come get me," I challenge, the roar of the wind muffling my shouts at the sky.

The rain strikes, stings, then tickles my skin.

"Hai," I say, releasing my repressed voice, my senses awakened.

In preparation for the rainy season, I stocked layers of wood along the triangle compartment on each side between the two angled slabs and the ground. I'm left with little room to maneuver except to sit on my rear end attending to the fire, lying down to sleep, and shimmying myself to collect water flowing off the rear-rock-wall into the den. I dodge the uneven ends of the stacked wood, careful not gouge an eye or poke my sore lower back. Each time my back throbs, I think, *My poor kidneys*. I assume the worst, with little margin for error. *Drink more water*. The firepit is between me and the exit. I use the small rock, which is one-fourth the height and a third the width of the entrance, as a buffer to the wind and rain, once used for cracking open the coconut. The fire flickers in the wind that blows rain over the rock buffer and through the entrance. I stick the end of coconut fronds into the sandy soil to shield the firepit. The implanted leaves hold steady and angle over the stones of one side of the firepit. Their hanging, pointed tips blacken and wilt away inches from the flames.

There's enough stacked wood outside the den to last through the rainy season. I cover them with a thick layer of leafed branches, coconut fronds on top of that, nearly sixty small to medium-sized rocks and stones to weigh down the fronds, and another layer of leafed branches for camouflage. The sogginess reaches inside the den, leaving my skin chilled and moist. The fire helps keep me and the den somewhat dry, but the amount of moisture overwhelms the effects of the fire. I pace my use of wood, careful that I'm not too frugal the fire dies out on me. I check and recheck, then check again, careful not to be caught off guard by fickle flames. The flow of water at the rear of the den cascades and collects in a growing puddle. I use the coconut cups to dig a wider opening at the bottom where each slab meets the soil along the cliff-wall. The water drains out, reducing the water level collected in the dip scoured out by the previous rainy seasons, and the reason why I've chosen to leave the firepit at the front near the entrance even though more exposed to the wind and rain.

Months of Rain

It never stops, I think, as I lie within the chilly dampness of the den amid the splash of endless raindrops. There's a saying that one can die from a thousand cuts. *What will billions of raindrops do to me?* It is as though I drink from a bottomless cup of water, at first quenching my thirst with refreshing, clean water on a hot day, then suffocating from the flow that never gives me a chance to catch my breath. As for food, it has found me. The rain brings out prey, whether a drenched bird grounded from its perch by the bombs of raindrops, the stray rat drowned out of its hole, or the snake in its element gliding across the flooded ground. I watch the puddles and flowing water outside the den while waiting for a break in the storm to venture further out. Each season, I'm reminded how persistent the pounding of rain and wind is during rainy season. It is much fiercer here than it is in Japan. I wait for the sun now and wait for the rain in summer. The never yielding sound of rain and wind are like the constant roar of the sea. *Oh, how I miss that scorching sun.*

***

A python slithers along the wet gloss atop the sandy soil like a sea serpent. I rush out of the den, the rain pricking me like pins. I jump in front of the snake. The python turns to avoid me, as I expected. I give chase and catch up to step on its tail. The snake swings around, attempting to bite me, which I also expected, but the thick-bodied python is not agile enough. If he were to face me in a dedicated challenge, I would stand down because this is when the otherwise docile python is dangerous. The snake, too big and strong to hold in place with my foot, escapes. While he gains momentum to glide away along the flooded ground, I rush back to the den, grabbing the bolo propped against the entrance. I catch up to the snake at the edge of the nook and cock my arm back. *I am samurai,* I think, striking down, cutting into his body. He hisses and attempts swinging around to face me. I jump on the opposite side while pulling the blade out and re-cocking my arm. I aim for the sliced-opened flesh from the previous strike.

"Banzai!" I say, fueling my strength as I chop down and cut through his thick, muscular body.

"Hai," I say, pleased from the proper kill of game, my racing heart replacing the tremble in my hands.

One less snake in the jungle. Time to feast.

My vision obscured by the rain running down my face, I cut a slit along the python's body on the large-rock-slab-table outside the den, then grab the two sides of the slits of hanging skin and pull off the skin by yanking on it as if I were pulling off a wet sock. The rain rinses the blood off the table. I do the same with the other half. After skinning the two halves, I string the meat along branches stuck in the ground to the side of the fire and leaning over the flames within the tight confines of the den. The snake cooks much like my clothes dry in the sun.

I breathe in the aroma of roasting snake to satisfy my waiting taste buds. I cut off chunks of meat as it cooks to test its readiness. It's a cross between fish and chicken, and a big step up from the tilapia. *How can such a menacing creature taste so good?* It makes the beetles taste like origami paper. The python is a gift from nature that should last me a few days, maybe more if I can keep it from spoiling by cooking it again and again to prevent bacteria from overtaking the meat. *I think that will work.*

To be a scientist was one of my many ambitions, as reading gave me an appetite to do and learn everything. My third-grade teacher, Ms. Suzuki, told me, "*Ni usagi wo ou mono wa ichi usagi wo mo ezu*" when I said I wanted to be a baseball player after claiming I would be a judo champion and teacher earlier in the school year. I didn't understand the depth of her statement at the time, but looking back on my life, it is clear. I agree with her sentiment that trying to do two things at once will make you fail in both. The military is one thing that I gave a singular focus to. At the time of fleeing, I achieved the rank of Lance Corporal. It was my profound comfort in a mind corralled of its many useless ambitions when the military consolidated my energy. A sense of purpose was born as a soldier. A purpose now lost in recognition of how much more was taken from me and my country rather than given.

***

The rain and wind call it quits after giving the jungle a thorough wash and filling the pond back up with water. The faint chatter of monkeys is first to awaken the jungle. The sunlit sky returns.

"Welcome back," I say.

Eager to bid farewell to the rain, I step out, squeezing every minute of the remaining day stretching in the open and absorbing sunlight. Mosquitoes emerge from the damp soil and create a cloud around me. A small pile of wood remains. *Success.*

A self-devouring stomach pang reminds me that no more time is to be wasted. I convince myself that danger of a passing plane no longer exists since the echoes of war vacated this part of the jungle. I creep out beyond the large tree and towards the edge of the nook, examining each bush and tree along the way, gathering fruit and nuts that were stripped away from their plants by wind and rain. I struggle to remember any of those plants I've passively learned in the years of my childhood adventures. *This looks familiar, that looks familiar*, I think one after another. Youthful curiosity attempts to resurface among a murky memory from a time of reckless experimenting with mysterious textures and tastes in nature.

> *Soon after starting primary school, and with more freedom, Shiro and I walked to and from the schoolhouse. We bypassed a weed-like plant lured by the appeal of red berries. We tried the berries. If we weren't so repulsed by the taste, we would have eaten more. That saved us. But we did get very sick, to the point we spent time in the hospital, where we were forced to empty our stomachs by vomiting. Those appealing* doku utsugi *berries were not ok to eat, and the weed-like* hikagehego *was ok to eat. Lesson learned.*

I sniff, rub, and suckle for any clues in my survey. *Be careful*, I think, as I always tell myself in my encounters since that childhood experience. In contrast to the average person, my caution with plants outweighs my caution with animals. *Does Shiro share my caution after having the same experience with the doku utsugi berries? I would think so.* I sift through my memories, not caring if I find the answer to a growing list of questions once I'm lost in the reverie.

Standing at the edge of the nook where the front-cliff-wall drops into the valley, I gaze into the distance, seeking clues of a lake or river. The thickness of the reinvigorated jungle hides many of the telltale signs. I climb down.

"Are you ok, Joe?" I ask, making sure that the topsoil hasn't washed away in the rain and exposed his remains.

I walk down the steep decline into the valley while choosing landmarks along the way that will direct me back, only to forget them minutes later. Malnutrition is taking a toll. My teeth are loosening.

> *"Supplies will be here soon," our sergeant kept telling us. "Have faith." Faith! If we relied on faith, we'd all be dead. We made great efforts to scavenge for our own food and had more faith in the Filipinos feeding us than we did in our superiors. We treated them like animals, yet they kept us alive. It's easier to say they feared what would happen to them if they let us starve, but I think kindness and generosity is in their nature. I like to think the average Japanese citizen would do the same. I'm forever jarred by the acts of cruelty of my comrades. This is not the Japanese way, I often told myself.*
>
> *We stopped to rest in the city of San Fernando during our long march to the prisoner camp at Capas Train Station, more than sixty miles away, in heat that dwarfs what I've experienced before and since. The direct assault of the sun was magnified by dehydration and the prodding of prisoners to march on. It was a test of everyone's endurance, with no mercy for the prisoners and little mercy given to us soldiers by our superiors. Many prisoners collapsed from exhaustion and were often killed instead of given a chance to rise. Seeing such disregard for life again and again numbed*

my sense of compassion.

As we rested on the main street leading into San Fernando from Bataan on the outskirts of the city, we soon realized we were in the heart of the Filipinos' version of Geisha Row where all prostitutes lived and provided services for both Filipino men and Japanese soldiers. In Tokyo, Geisha Row was a street where most of the geisha houses were located on the south side of the city. Unlike the bright paint and well-constructed homes and buildings of Geisha Row, here the buildings were one-level wood shacks lining the street. They combined living quarters for the women at the rear with an open-air restaurant at the front.

Although exhausted, my comrades vanished into these building one by one. When our battalion commander, Major Ueno, found some of his soldiers missing, he ordered everyone out of the buildings. My comrades emerged side by side with the women, about fifty people in total. All my comrades carried their rifles, but many of them were half-clothed.

"Get back in there and get dressed," he demanded of the soldiers not fully dressed.

When they returned fully clothed, he ordered the guilty men to step forward.

"Turn around and face your woman," he said.

The men turn, looking eye to eye with the women they had just been in company with.

"Raise your rifle."

The men raised their rifles, aiming the nose of the rifles downward towards the ground.

"Place the tip of your rifle between the eyes of the women."

The men are slow to do so. The cries of the women cascade

over the silence as everyone there stays frozen in the moment, watching.

"Do not take your eyes off these women," he demanded. "What do you see? A frightened woman? Can you feel their fear?"

One soldier turns away, trying to look back to Major Ueno.

"Don't look away, Private Fumihiro!"

The man is quick to set his sight back on the woman before him.

My eyes focused on the woman, tears glistening along the curves of her cheeks. Her face was deformed with what I'm guessing were birth defects of ears made up of holes on the side of her head minus earlobes. I thought of how her life of enduring ridicule had led her to that moment. In these brothels, she'd found the attention of men that was missing most of her life, and her defects made her more expendable to Major Ueno.

"Shoot!" Major Ueno demands. "Damnit, Private Fimuhiro! Shoot!" I turn away.

Bang!

"Never neglect your duties," Major Ueno said before walking away. In that moment, "This is not the Japanese way" resonated strongest.

I look back to the mountain peak through the spacing of the trees behind me, careful not to lose my bearings. I lunge forward deeper into the jungle thickness. My arms and rifle are held high to protect my face from the sharp points of branches. In a relative clearing, vines hang from a tree and collect on the ground around it. *Rope*, should I need some.

Something breathes like an old, overweight man climbing stairs. There, behind some bushes, a dark image. I squint. The wild pig snorts and sniffs the ground. My eyes are wide and my mouth waters as I imagine the golden-crisp skin and clumps of roasted meat clinging to it, all seasoned with the oils of its melted fat. I remove the rifle from my shoulder with its bayonet already attached. The pig's heavy breathing is accompanied by snorts as his way of saying, "I found something to nibble on." I approach with a bush shielding me from sight, inching my way closer, watching my steps and careful not to warn the pig with the crunch of leaves or snap of a twig. I reach the bush. The pig sniffs, snorts on the other side. I take my hand off the trigger and wrap the rifle's strap around my wrist, preparing to plunge the bayonet into the pig through a gap within the thinned-leafed branches of the bush. As soon as I see the pig's head emerge in view through the gap, I thrust the blade towards its neck. The rifle snags on the branches and the pig runs off squealing without my blade ever reaching him. I aim at the running pig. The weight of the bayonet sways my aim at the shrinking figure. Pop! The gunshot echoing as if it is the only sound in the jungle. The pig disappears into the thickets. It's quiet. *I got him*.

When I break through the thicket wall he ran into, the pig is gone and there's no trace of blood. *Another failure.* My concern turns to those gunshot echoes. I scan the valley in all directions before turning my attention to where the pig was snorting the ground. A common grass grows near the base of the bushes. *If the pig can eat it, I can.* I nibble on the bland, moist grass before returning to the den. *New food*, I think. It is something I never thought to turn to. The nook is full of this grass.

***

Today, I walk further into the jungle. Ahead is a large, open clearing with the sunlight brightening that part of the jungle floor. The charm of birds is sparse as I continue to walk towards the clearing. I slow my stride on sight of the first clean-lined structure of huts camouflaged by the overgrowth of foliage. These weathered bamboo huts are a hybrid, their material created by the hands of nature but joined in a pattern by the hands of man. Each hut's plot is like their own little island in an archipelago of islands, as the trees and bushes are free to grow as they choose. I creep up behind a tree at the clearing's edge, look down into the village, and listen. No people or animals roam the streets, no chickens cackle, and a window creaks while shuddering in the breeze. *Where did everyone go?* I shiver due to the eeriness. *Wiped-out, extinguished,* I think.

I go from hut to hut, trying to salvage what I can, bracing myself to see mutilated bodies. The village is already stripped of anything with value. I find an opened, rusty tin can with its sharp-edged lid bent back. *Trash to others, treasure for me. Perfect to store my embers.* The heat of the firepit will warm the inside of the tin long after the fire is out, and I'll punch holes through the tin so as not to extinguish the embers from a lack of oxygen. This man-made item will aid in my survival. Although it is much like the cold, industrial steel of my rifle and contrasting with the jungle.

> *On some days, Shiro and I came back from the jungle with burlap sacks of cans and bottles to make a little money to buy candy or play at the arcade. There was a store down the street from us that all the neighborhood kids frequented because they sold the best* yatsuhashi, uiro, sakuramochi,

> *and imported candy bars from America. My favorite was the thin chocolate bars attached together in four sections with wafers inside. At the front of the store were arcade games which often took most of our money, as we easily lost track of what we spent. We put coins in the machine to begin and wouldn't think twice before putting more coins in to start the next game. We played until we ran out of money, which was the reason why we bought our candy first and played the arcade games with what remained, so we didn't leave the place without satisfying our insatiable adolescent sweet tooths. Pachinko was my favorite game, as I watched the small metal balls drop one by one to realize their fate as each zig-zagged over the dark-blue background with artwork of a beady-eyed samurai and exploding fireworks. Recycling cans and bottles was the primary way we funded our play and treats.*

Animal, I think, seeing movement out of the corner of my eye. A dog the size of a pig runs into the street. It reminds me of Hachikō, an Akita Inu I had in Japan, except Hachikō had one ear flopped-over.

"Come here," I call, clicking with my tongue.

I move closer, slouching over and rubbing the tips of my fingers as if there was something to give. The dog stares at my hand and tilts his head. His tail wags. I creep my hand back towards my bolo, shifting the dog's attention away from my rubbing fingers. He lowers his head and growls. *Friend or food?* My mind jostles between the two before my next move. I draw and swing my bolo in one efficient motion. He leaps backwards, and much like the wild pig, the dog squeals as I swipe at him. He runs off. *But I love dogs,* I tell myself. *Survival,* I convince myself, out of guilt.

"Come here," I call out, looking for him as though he will sense my apologetic tone.

The dog is nowhere to be seen.

In the center of the village, along the main street, is a water pump for an old well. The lever is light and loose as I first start pumping, but as I continue, the tension increases. Water trickles out, then brown water flows. I pump until the water clears, drink, rinse out the tin, then wash my hands and face. As the water runs off my face and blurs my vision, a small man stands at the end of the main street. I rush to wipe the water from my face while snatching up my rifle. When I look back down the road, the man is gone. I pick up the tin and trek back to my den, thinking what is to come of the man spotting me. The discomfort of the mosquitoes nagging me all day pales in comparison to my worry.

***

A chilly discomfort wakes me in the middle of the night. I fall back to sleep, then wake again, coughing over the nocturnal sounds, with a throbbing head and a sheen of sweat over my entire body. Falling in and out of sleep with my body weak, my arms and legs sprawl over the sandy soil and my eyes flutter in a struggle to sleep through the discomfort. The nighttime coolness brings me relative comfort. By morning, my canteen is half empty. The prospect of death hits me, as I do not possess the strength or wherewithal to boil water. Recognizing the dire need for water is the extent of my progress toward ever obtaining some.

I fall in and out of consciousness, unable to suppress my cough from echoing. With much effort, I sip from my canteen at regular intervals until it is empty. The day's heat magnifies the fever to where my sweating body is like a wet rag squeezed of its water. Sickness rots me from the inside out. Slow and steady, it feels like a vice squeezes my body. My vision blurs. The sunlight and colors of the jungle become a piece of smudged artwork within my mind's conscious and unconscious states, as if I'd taken a hallucinogenic. *Am I dreaming? Am I awake?*

The chirp of a bird is like a whistle in my ear, the leaves rattling in the breeze are like bells tolling, and the buzzing of insects is like the roar of a jet plane. Ghostlike images dance by me or charge at me from all angles. People from my past are there with me. The den walls become the bamboo walls of my childhood home. My wife Tamiko is here with me, preparing a cup of tea and kneeling next to me. She coddles the teacup against my lips. I sip, feeling her gentle hand guide my head towards the cup. The blur of my eyesight clears for a moment, and the vision of Tamiko is replaced by a woman holding my head up.

"Mama. Papa," I mumble.

I drink from the coconut cup. A dark-skinned woman smiles at me. A small, dark-skinned man stands behind her near the entrance, wearing a loincloth and holding a spear as though it's an extension of his arm. They speak an unrecognizable language, with the man's short stature evident by his ability to stand inside the den without crouching over.

I'm tickled by breath on my neck and shift my eyes in that direction. *Hachikō?* I think, brought back to my convoluted reality. *But Hachikō is dead.* Then, once again grounded in the present by that thought, I recognize the dog as the same dog I saw, befriended, and tried to slay in the deserted village. He sniffs at me.

Forgiving or forgetful, he licks my face. *Good dog,* I think, wishing I could reciprocate the affection. If it weren't for the presence of the man and woman, maybe he'd bite a chunk off the side of my face.

"You were willing to take a bite out of me," he would say.

Unable to hold my eyes open any longer, I fall asleep.

I wake early, nauseous, feverous, and with a dose of strength. The fire crackles with a collection of small flames at its heart of charred and glowing red logs, despite me not tending to it. A cup full of shaved pieces of tree bark sits on the small-rock-table at my feet. *It wasn't a dream.* I'm quick to swivel my head to scan around me, then muster the strength to get up. I sit on my rear end, grab my rifle, and stay there guarding the entrance. *Someone knows I'm here,* I think, my hands trembling. Scanning for any movement in the nook, my finger holds the trigger so firm that if I had cleaned the rifle of all the dirt and grime, the trigger would collapse from the tension and a shot would ring out.

After about ten minutes, with that spurt of adrenaline gone, my body collapses and I have no qualms about resting in the twisted position where I lie. Extreme weakness has resolved my concern, or at least any action to address it. My heart races, then eases, races, then eases., the spurts of panic unsustainable within a weary body and mind.

I wake at night to the clogged breathing of my own heavy snoring. No fever, head no longer throbbing, chill gone, but my muscles ache in a state of spirit-sucking fatigue. *How long was I asleep?* I remember at least two different moons. The dark faces of the man and woman, the woman's gentle touch, and the man's earthy musk dominate my Delphic consciousness. *People.* I am warmed by the thought. *Kind, gentle people.*

I fall back to sleep and wake with the sun prominent in the sky, the heat mild and the breeze cooling me within the shade of the den. The soreness in my muscles and a dry mouth persist. My strength and spirit return at the pace of an uncoiling cherry blossom in March. I reach for my canteen to find it full of water. I drink, and as my lips catch the flowing water, my eyes lock on to a bamboo culm about eight inches long, standing tall on its end, and a banana leaf stuffed into the other end.

"Thank you," I say as if the man and woman are there in the den with me.

I put down the canteen and pick up the warm bamboo culm, darkened brown from the fire, tilt it sideways, and pull on the edge of the banana leaf. Two banana leaf bundles slide out. Each is filled with a serving of rice and chicken—a restaurant-like luxury well beyond any imaginable expectation in my situation. I insert one banana leaf bundle back into the bamboo culm for later but waste no time eating the first. I must have broken a record eating that first wrap, if records were kept on such a trivial thing. *Trivial! Nothing trivial about that. I desperately needed it.* As I wash down the last bits of chicken and rice with water from the canteen, I freeze at the sight of a rasorial hen passing the entrance of the den—casual, cackling, while picking at the ground with her beak. I squeeze my eyes closed and rattle my head, before reopening my eyes to confirm I'm not hallucinating.

"Would you look at that," I say.

I glance over to my rifle. It's out of reach. I look back to the hen. Leaning forward on my knees, I prepare to leap and grab it as it clucks in and out of sight outside the entrance. The hen turns to look at me and then continues to cluck and peck at the ground.

"Cockle-doodle-do," adds a rooster from the other side of the den wall.

More chickens! I relax from my planned pounce and exit the den to find a rooster, two hens, and a covered bamboo basket full of chicken feed. The feed is comprised of small bits of split, old, dry, unwashed grains that I would eat if there weren't a full burlap bag of rice placed along the outer den wall. *I must thank them,* I think, in the guilt of knowing how valuable all of this is.

"Thank you," I say to them, looking south towards the village where I believe they live.

I also find the bark and remaining leaves of the *dita* tree, used for the tea that healed me of malaria, on the large-rock-slab-table. Reflecting back to the man and woman's dark skin and short stature, it dawns on me, *they are Aetas.*

> *I was assigned to lead a group to collect more coconuts.*
> *"What's out that way?" I asked a villager while pointing towards a dense part of the jungle.*
> *"The jungle, Po," he told me.*
> *"Coconuts?"*
> *"Probably coconuts and Aetas, Po," he told me.*
> *"Aetas?" I asked, assuming he would describe some fruit.*
> *"The natives," he said, and pointed to his ten-year-old son.*
> *"Short as him," he added, refusing to use his son's name in fear of us knowing the boy better, "and black, Po." He rubbed his finger along the skin of his arm and face.*
> *At that point, I recalled what we'd been told by our superiors about the Aetas, who they referred to as the "black natives."*
> *"They are, for the most part, neutral. Stewards of the jungle and part of the jungle. Use their help when you can," Warrant Officer Ito said, while giving us tips before our assault on the island.*

Days Later

My first order of business this morning, now that my strength is back, is to wrangle a chicken or two. *Yakitori*. This time with chicken, as it's supposed to be. I suspect returning to beetle yakitori will not be so easy after chicken yakitori. The thought is nearly as tantalizing as the crisp, roasted pig that never came to be. I focus on the hen most oblivious to my movements. Even as the other chickens flap away, the hen is slow to react, focused on plucking chicken feed tossed onto the sandy soil. *Is this one stupid?* Despite what looks like an easy catch, my attention turns to the rooster for the reward of a bigger meal.

"You're dinner today," I say, as I move towards the rooster. "Come here, mister."

I lick my lips and gulp at the thought much like the exaggerated reaction of a *kyōgen* actor. I chase the rooster into the corner against the rear -rock-wall and den wall. He postures for a showdown. I crouch down with arms extended, as if spreading wings to keep him from escaping.

"Gotcha," I tell him.

We're face-to-face. The rooster turns from a mild-mannered domesticated bird into a fierce, defiant one and squawks at me, prepared to gouge my eyes out with his beak. I take a small step back. *It's just a chicken*, I think, stepping forward. I look him dead in the eyes.

"Banzai!" I cry, lunging forward.

The rooster hops high into the air, trying to fly over me. I take a big step back, keeping him between me and the walls. I lunge at him again. Flapping his wings, he attempts to fly over the slanted wall of the den and to the other side. Nearly over the top, at the apex of adjoining slabs of rocks, I reach out, grab a leg, and yank him back down and secure his legs. His wings flap in my grip before I begin prepping the chicken and inserting a stick down the middle of the carcass. Once placed over the fire out of the reach of the flames, I rotate the chicken a few inches about every fifteen minutes, while roasting the liver and kidneys on another stick. I stuff a handful of rice into the bamboo culm sealed by a node at one end, add water, and seal the open end by stuffing a wet banana leaf into it. *Bananas,* I realize after using the leaf. *Where can I find these bananas?* I place the culm in the firepit like I found it a few days ago. The heat and water sealed in the bamboo culm steams the rice inside.

"Done," I say, slapping my hands together. After finishing half the chicken and rice, I lie down and stretch out. My stomach sinks when I realize my error. I have two hens remaining with no male. *Stupid me.* I slap the heel of my palm against my forehead. I was so quick to judge the hen who's now feeding and clucking on the ground around my head, in my den.

***

I carve a wooden figurine of Buddha and place it on the rock-slab-table, on top of the banana leaf used to wrap the chicken and rice. *A token of appreciation*. When the day comes I meet the Aeta couple, I'll explain Buddha's meaning. I will tell them about *Kami* too. It is said *Kami* is everywhere and in everything in nature. It is probably closest to what they believe. I can also learn from the Aetas about what they believe since their ancestors were here long before names like Bataan or Philippines were assigned to the land. I do not fear them or question their intentions, only that word will spread with a single careless mention of my presence. I'm relying on their discretion. My life depends on it. I expect to see the Aeta couple lurking in the bushes or wake to a fresh supply of goods. *Where are my new friends?*

One month passes. *Why wouldn't they return to check on me?* The figurine remains in the same spot, starting to weather and crack from the sun. *Trouble,* my instinct tells me. I gather my gear and climb onto one of those stair-like niches on the rear-rock-wall that looks down into the nook and spend most nights there, only returning to the nook when I need to boil more water and dig up more *kamotes*.

The tin has kept the embers well, and I've been carrying it with me and blowing on it a few times a day to get the dying embers to glow bright. I expect the Aetas to emerge through the barrier of trees, or perhaps a Filipino scout. *Spear or rifle?* I repeat this in my head all day, every day, for three weeks of heightened caution before returning to live in the den, driven more by reaching the limit of eating uncooked insects collected in and around the niche.

***

A thin, smoky fog spreads through the valley floor. The smoke prompts me to venture out beyond the barrier and seek out my friends. I venture out during the day and return at night for six consecutive days, focusing on the area around the abandoned village where I first saw the Aeta man and his dog. I'm tempted to give them all names. *Who am I to name them?* I'm also afraid that I will get so used to the made-up names, I wouldn't call them by their real ones if I met them. *When. When I do meet them.*

On the third day, I follow a trail well beyond the village and to the foothills of the adjacent mountain range, where I find a charred plot of land with the remains of a smoldering hut. The red Huk flag hangs on a nearby tree as a warning to others. I inspect the site inch by inch, flipping through the charred debris, fingers and arms blackened. Digging through a pile of debris in the center of what used to be the hut, I'm overcome with an intense chill upon finding two charred bodies covered by debris. *No, please no,* I think, and clear all debris off the bodies. Although the bodies are burnt beyond recognition, find the iron tip of the Aeta man's spear next to the bodies. My legs give way and I drop to my knees. *Those damn Huks,* I think, while clenching the spearhead and holding it over my heart.

"*Arigatou*," I say, bowing my head.

I create a shared burial for the couple and place a rock for a headstone.

Standing next to the gravesite, hand over heart, I say, "Be at peace, my friends. I will not forget you. Your harmony and sublimity are forever."

At the nook, I hammer the spearhead into the large, old tree to serve as a cenotaph.

I toss and turn all night. *Damn Huks.* "I will find justice for you, my friends," I say, looking to the trees around me, anger building like the steam within my canteen placed over the fire. *Uncorrupted hearts.* I think about the Aetas and how war jaded the rest of us. I'm ready for a confrontation to defend the honor of the Aetas and the ways of the jungle. *Let the Huks find me.*

"Enough innocent lives!" I say, flushing out my inhibitions.

***

A rainbow streaks across the valley from the mist of a passing cloud. I study the colors, matching the different hues within the landscape with many unique colors within the scope of my sight. In this brief time of viewing the rainbow, I'm enlightened to the beauty of light in the prismatic display and dwell on the importance of water to this beauty. It appears coordinated to help me find some solace in my grief, with the *koto* playing in my head for the remainder of the day. With contentment, I set fresh ears and eyes on the jungle—the howling and chattering of monkeys wild at play in the distance, the exotic birds with their own unusual song and dance, the sweetness replacing all rankness in the air, and the warm, sandy soil between my toes. *Kami*, I think, sensing it here and now as though guiding me to the truth. The idea of dying here, immersed in nature, is a more peaceful prospect than among the murky and misguided values of man.

I stand on the ledge above Joe.

"Hi, my friend," I say, looking down at the gravesite, contemplating the same possible fate as him.

I sought solace in nature as a child, and I do so now, as my mind migrates further from war and memories of loved ones. *My past is my past. It does not help me. I must learn to provide for myself. Tomorrow is not set.* The young, mysterious Filipina girl continues to visit me in my dreams. Sometimes she reaches for me, sometimes I reach for her.

Years 2 and 3

I lie flat on my back with a beard thick enough to cover that scar across my face. The bars of my ribs press well-defined against the skin and rise above the concave of my belly. *I need more protein.* I survive on mostly insects, the occasional *kamote*, grass, new batches of coconuts growing on the tree every few months and then eventually falling to the ground or rotting up there in the tree. One of my best finds so far is a cashew tree. I pluck a handful of the yellow cashew apple, return to the den, remove the cashew shell from the apple, burn the shell over the fire, then crack open the shell, removing the cashew nut. I eat the roasted cashews, then suck the juice from the mango-like flesh of the fruit, which tastes like a combination of cashew and mango. But it is the protein from

the nuts that's most beneficial to me. I enjoy two cashew apples and save the rest for the next few days. All this is provided within a limited radius from the base of the nook. My area of free-range expands from the safety of the nook, but I remain on heightened guard since finding the Aetas' charred bodies almost a year ago—my unsettled nerves urging me towards revenge against the Huks.

"Come on. Find me," I say, slapping my fist against my chest.

My heart beats fast. The cool night's breeze blows over me. *I'm safe here.* My heartbeat slows in rhythm to the chirping crickets.

"Kaiyo," the Aeta woman calls out.

I swing the bolo, slicing through a corn stalk, then look her way. The couple stands at the entrance of their hut.

"Come, eat. We are waiting for you."

I spear the bolo into the soil before walking over. When I enter, the couple is not there.

"Hello?" I call out to them.

An unwrapped banana leaf of streaming rice and chicken rests on a small table.

"Hello?" I call out again, before kneeling next to the small table.

I eat, finishing the rice and swallowing the chicken meat and bones. "Thank you," I call out.

I wait and listen for someone to respond and turn to face the entrance while remaining on my knees.

A man enters with a red bandana around his forehead.

"Let's talk," he says, waving me to follow him outside.

I rise from my knees and exit the hut. The man stands next to the gravesites of the Aetas.

"This is your fault," he tells me. Angered, I yell, "You killed them."

"If you took good care of yourself, they'd still be alive."

I run over to the bolo sticking out of the ground, pick it up, and charge at the man. He stands there, waits for me, and I swing the bolo, chopping him down as if he were another corn stalk.

The man, covered in blood, looks up to me, "Do you feel better?"

I drop the bolo onto the ground and stare at my bloody hands.

I wake, lie still, then raise my dirt-brown, calloused hands before my face, relieved it's not reality.

***

Where are the mangoes? Where are the bananas? Where is the meat? Any meat. That's what I crave, that's what I need. Meat! The rustle of bushes in the breeze brings a flash of hope that another wild pig sniffs and snorts behind them. Of all the insects, it's the crickets that I'm fond of, cooked with a squirt of calamansi juice. Crickets are not plentiful, but I collect them from a patch of drying grass here in the nook.

Those varmints remain elusive, catching only quick sight of a scurrying mouse once. The cobra lasts two days at the most after roasting. I roast one-third of the python meat before boiling the rest as a stew, which extends its life by another day or two, up to a total of five days. I use what I collect, eating the fruit of the cashew and reusing the shells of the coconuts, cutting from all the rising blades of edible grass within the nook but leaving enough for them to quickly grow back, swallowing the calamansi whole after squeezing the juice over my crickets, and eating more than enough of the less sought-after insects. I also eat the skin, leaves, and roots of the *kamote*. The jungle holds everything one needs, but I have yet to learn of it all.

I find another patch of dry grass. Crickets hop around in a frenzy, as if I were looking down on the streets of Tokyo from high above. I place the canteen in the center of the plot of grass with a small amount of water left inside. Returning the next day, a handful of crickets who crawled in for a drink but couldn't find their way back out remain in the canteen, many using the light from the opening to guide them out. Shiro and I used clear glass bottles.

We thought we were geniuses and could make millions selling a cricket trap to the world.

"Mr. Kenji, the glassmaker. He can make custom bottles for us," Shiro proposed.

"Why don't we just recycle old bottles?"

"Then people will just copy us. We don't want to let people know that a regular bottle works. We want them to think that only our bottle works. That our bottle is special, magic."

"Put a label on it. Magic Cricket Bottle. That's what we'll call it," I responded, as if I was responsible for the whole id ea. "We'll travel the world. Okinawa. Hawaii. Hollywood," Shiro said.

Using a decaying, frequently reused banana leaf as a glove, I lift the hot stone, quick to drop the stone on the soil, and squeeze calamansi juice over the crickets as they sizzle. Unlike the coconut fronds, banana leaves have no gaps. It's like coconut fronds are stitched fabric and banana leaves are leather. I turn my attention back to the crunchy tartness of the crickets, picking out every little piece of cricket caught between my teeth with my tongue and finger, then sucking on the pieces collected by my tongue.

The light of a full moon seeps through the cleft. My stomach gurgles and moans, the taste of crickets and calamansi remaining on my tongue. Mosquitoes delay my sleep. I swat at them, hoping to crush the pests between my hand and face, slapping an empty hand against my face more often than catching one of them. *I look foolish. Good thing no one is watching. They would think I'm delusional. That I've lost my mind, swatting the empty air.* I slap away.

***

I cling to the reverie of family and friends which threatens to slip from my grip. *The laughter of Maeko in the next room as her mother reads to her, Tamiko stroking my stubbled chin as she comforts me in bed the first night after returning from basic training, the jab of Shiro's fist to my shoulder after first finding out Tamiko and I kissed.* These memories fight to the surface for a breath of air before being drowned out by memories of those souls lost in war or those people forever corrupted by it. I will die here, alone, my impending death inconsequential. Justice for my part in all wrongs served. Regrets nag. *What should I have done differently with my life? Will Maeko ever forgive me?* But it's war that plagues me most right now. *How can I put that behind me and move on? Pop! Bang! Boom! Pop! Pop! Pop!* The routine and familiarity with my surroundings softens those haunting sounds and images. *I stood by. I did nothing. Tamiko. Maeko. Tamiko. Maeko.* But I cannot deny my mind revisiting those screams and terrified faces in war. I'm distant from it but no longer numb to it. It is like the bastion of solitude has awoken a dormant part of my soul imprisoned by war. *What has my life become? What have I become?* The war will end, but accountability for my actions or inactions will never cease. *Is that the real me?* My place in the world as a soldier and father is frail. Self-doubt rots my mind like malaria did my body.

My uniform is ripped, worn thin, and hangs from my body like drying moss hanging from the tips of branches, my boots falling apart with the leather detaching from the uneven wear of the rubber soles. I remove my clothes, toss my boots aside, cut the fabric of my clothes into long swathes, tie the cloth together into one long piece, and wrap it around my torso as a loincloth just like my Aeta friend wore. My bare, callused feet more comfortable than the unstable footing in the tattered boots. I walk the trails with ease. *I am Aeta,* able to cast away all other titles.

***

The monkeys chatter. *Monkey meat.* I climb down the cliff and make my way in the direction of the monkeys, using their howls to guide me until I see blotches of their brown and black fur among the treetops. When I'm close enough to see the gray of the fur on the macaques' underbellies, they scream as if a territorial line was crossed. I stop and swing the rifle strap over my shoulder, hiding the rifle behind me. They carry on. I near a young macaque who strayed far from the group and moves along the branches, naïve to me watching her. I click my tongue. She flinches and looks over to me, then carries on crawling along the branch. *This may be my chance.* I remove the rifle from my shoulder. They scream. *Shoot now?* But I take steps backwards until they calm, removing myself from taking a

clear shot, and sit at the edge of their playground. The young macaques are drawn away from their family in fixation on me. They play again, swinging from and climbing on paths along the branches, as if in performance for me. *"Have fun,"* I whisper to them and watch all day without the thought of raising my rifle.

Months

The playful chatter of macaques in the nook wakes me. Exiting the den, they're jolted by my approach, frozen at the sight of me, and prepare to flee. I kneel, observe. They resume their chatter and play. The little ones jump onto and slide off the wide base of the coconut tree in failed attempts to climb it. The alpha climbs by cupping its hands along the backside of the tree and walking up the trunk, making it seem as if he's not hindered by gravity.

"You make it look so easy," I say, talking softly to myself.

Reaching the batch of coconuts, he pulls one off its stem. *These are my coconuts.* The alpha climbs to the very top, sits there in a nest-like perch, and yanks at the thick, fibrous outer layer of the coconut using his jaws and hands.

"Go," I say, clapping my hands to startle the pod.

They scatter, leaving the large male atop the tree alone. I lead them away from the nook. When they stop to look back at me, I clap my hands again to urge them along, as if they are a herd of goats. Away from the nook, an adult female corrals the younger ones while the older males sit along the outer edges of the pod. They all play, groom one another, observe me, and are startled by any rustle, snap, or buzz. The alpha rejoins the pod after finishing the coconut in privacy. *You're welcome*, I think, looking at his smug face. I stay in their company until late afternoon and create little distraction with my departure when I sneak back to the den before sunset, finding the cleaned-out coconut shell near the base of the tree.

Before turning in for the night, I hop onto the tree and attempt to imitate the alpha macaque. My feet do not grip the tree enough and I slide off. Eager to try, and with enough sunlight remaining, I make the trek to collect from those hanging rattan vines found over a year ago. When I return to the coconut tree, dusk has set in. *I waited long enough to conquer this.* Wrapping a bundle of small vines around my ankles in a single loop, I use the grip of the vines against the tree to press me upward. My feet and legs move much like how a frog leaps, all working in unison with each push or hop up the tree. My arms assist with some of the upward momentum, but used mostly for balance. After reaching the top, breathless, leg and arm muscles burning, I chop the coconuts off their stem. They vanish in the darkness and thud onto the ground in a single bunch. *Victory.* I store my harvest inside the den and will ration them out over the coming weeks. It is not until morning that I look closely at their hard, green shells. They will provide plenty of milk but less of the tasty white flesh. I will wait until they are brown for the next harvest to feast on the copra.

***

A rustle among the fallen leaves wakes me from a midday nap. My eyes shoot open and pupils adjust. My view is onto the smooth surface of the slanted-rock-slab-wall in front of me, sand embedded into its dark gray composite, sparkling in the mild morning light which is seeping into the den. I listen. My senses tuned, and with a slight tilt of my head, I position my ear toward the exit. I gauge the proximity of the sound, calibrating the planned angle of sight, before shooting my head sideways to peer out. My eyes fixate on a blurred overview of the jungle and adjust to the new depth of field. Within this perceptual canvas, the rustling sound draws my attention to the center of a bed of leaves collected on the ground.

A bayawak pops its head out above the dry-fluffed leaves like the scope of a submarine. I inch my way to one knee, then two, while at the same time reaching for my rifle. I open the chamber of the rifle to confirm it's loaded, close it, then raise the rifle, aiming it towards movement under the leaves where the lizard has buried his head again. The pop of unlocking the safety on the rifle causes him to shoot out from the bed of leaves to reveal his stout front legs slightly turned in towards each other as though pigeon-toed. The length of his body from nose to tail tip is nearly a yard long. With head held high in alertness and tongue licking the air, the bayawak shimmies left, then right, then left again. It scurries to a nearby tree, claws crackling against the bark as it climbs.

The lizard now sits perched on a low branch, head darting left to right, sensing my presence with his tongue. I keep my eyes set on him as I reach down to my knapsack and glance at the remaining bullets before peering back up and locking eyes onto the bayawak. I set the rifle on the ground and remove the bolo dangling under my left armpit from a holder made of leather from my tattered boots and a rattan vine strap. I crawl out of the den on all fours. The lizard shoots a few inches further up the branch before pausing again. I lift myself up to one knee, then slowly rise to my feet and tiptoe towards him. The bayawak scurries along the branch another couple of feet. I pause, he pauses.

I sneak across the dry soil in long, gentle strides, avoiding the crunch of scattered leaves. Recognizing that the lizard's only escape route is to come back down the way he went up, I sprint across the crunching leaves to the base of the tree. His escape route is sealed, and my intent no longer a mystery to him. The bayawak jets to the end of the branch. I'm drawn that way by instinct, as it's become a face-off of wits, but this move brings me a few steps further away from the base of the tree. He zips back down the branch and then down the tree. I jump toward him and take a swipe at the lizard with the bolo as he runs down the tree. He avoids the strike by leaping off, and the blade chops into the tree. The bayawak glides along the ground with a stiff upper body, legs churning under the layer of leaves, giving the illusion he's floating. He runs down the slight slope of the nook into a maze of rocks which are part of the front-cliff-wall.

Outwitted! I throw the bolo at the nearest tree in a fit. It clangs and bounces off the tree onto the ground and vanishes into the bed of leaves.

"So close, you monster, you reptile," I say, clenching my empty hands and staring at them.

As a young boy, I made my way along the edge of the raised pathway where the tree stood centered among the rice paddies. Near the pathway was an irrigation canal with stagnant water yet to be released into the field. After rigging up the fishing line, I dropped the lure into the canal and sat against the cherry blossom tree while I waited. It wasn't more than ten seconds after sitting down that I felt a tug on the line. I drew in the line, much like pulling a small boat by its rope onto shore. As I hoisted the frog out of the water and over the embankment, his legs flailed as if climbing air while he swayed side to side on the line. When close enough, I grabbed the frog around his belly to unhook him and place him in a burlap sack. Each time I cast the line back in, a frog took the bait as quickly as the first time. I stopped at nine and brought home the burlap sack full of frogs.

"A gift for you, Mama," I said, holding up the sack of jostling frogs.

My mother took a step back and said, "Is that a snake?"

"Frogs, Mama."

She took a step closer to me, grabbed the bag, looked inside, and smiled.

I did the same years to follow, my mother's smile shrinking each time until her reaction became a blank stare and my frog catching stopped.

***

Mosquitoes nag and poke at every surface of my exposed skin. Their buzzes echo in my ear like the drone of tiny airplanes, my earlobe the canyon over which they fly. I slap, blow, and shake my way through the constant haze of these pestering insects swarming in a cloud around me. I use a coconut frond to swat them away, cutting through the haze before the mosquitoes regather and once again swarm. They jockey with each move I make. I scoop up moist leaves weighing heavy against the ground and add them to the fire. The haze of mosquitoes thins and is replaced by the thick haze of the smoke. I cover my face as the smoke vents out the den and up above the treetops. It permeates into my dwelling, masking the smell of my sweat and breath. I cough, tolerating the smoke until there's no more buzzing around me. I wait, breathing in the air lower to the ground and hoping the pests forget about me as I smother the flames with sand. Only a small group of mosquitoes pester me late at night when I'm deep in sleep. *There must be a better solution. Surrender?*

> *Aside from her father, mosquitoes kept Tamiko cooped up in her home. "Is it my blood type?" she asked.*
> *"What is your blood type?" "How would I know?"*
> *"I think it's more odor than blood type. Maybe it's the perfume you wear," I suggested.*
> *"You mean my Soir de Paris that I rarely wear? I thought you liked it."*
> *"I do but maybe the mosquitoes do too."*
> *She stopped using the perfume for three months, to no avail.*
> *"Maybe it is your blood type," I said, to annoy her.*

***

Collecting more coconut fronds to use in and around the den, I find an unusual, large beetle among them. This beetle is adorned with a rhinoceros-like snout and reddish-brown hair on her back. I bring the beetle and fronds to the den. I tie a string, made from the thread of cloth, to the center of the beetle's body to keep her from escaping. She waddles around the den, spreading her wings as if contemplating flying away, then pulls them in. I watch her explore the confines of the den with the end of the string wrapped around my finger.

"Come on, let me see you fly," I murmur, wishing to see the spectacle of small wings lifting her large, clunky body into the air.

I poke her, urging her to fly. She regains her balance, crawls over the coconut tree frond-covered floor of the den, then rests between the layers. I tug the string, pulling her closer to the edge of the frond she hides under. She crawls deeper into the pile of stacked fronds. I lie and wait, hoping she will emerge on her own. She is idle under the cover, as though taking an afternoon nap. I close my eyes, string still wrapped around my finger. My mind wanders, curious about what else hides among these fronds. I imagine tiny worms or hairless caterpillars on me. I shiver and itch to the thought. Turning towards her, I take a short nap while I wait.

When I wake, she remains hidden. I pull on her, one small tug after another, until she is out from under the fronds. Finding herself in the open and as if I woke her from a deep sleep, she begins moving again. She crawls towards me. I pull her up off the ground with the string.

"Fly," I say, bouncing her up and down in the air like a yo-yo.

She dangles, feet still moving as though she's forgotten how to fly. "Are you ok?" I ask, examining her for injuries.

I toss the beetle up in the air while holding the end of the string. She flies. The string extends and the tension tightens as she pulls away then hovers when there is no more give in the string. I pull on it like the reins of a horse, leading her as she flies in circles, me spinning along. Entertained by it all, I rein her in closer with each circle and snatch the beetle out of the air. I tie the end of the string to a small rock as though she is a horse in a stable. She crawls back into the pile of fronds with the slack given. "Make yourself comfortable," I tell her.

Hours later, among the idleness within the den, she re-emerges, crawling along the sandy soil towards the den's entrance until reaching the end of her line. The beetle's feet dig as she tries to walk further against the tension of the string. Her legs stop churning and she stays there in the open at the triangle of the entrance. On the other side is the stir of midday. The constant gaze of the jungle is upon her just as it is upon me. What eyes have or will set sight on her worries me.

What devours beetles? You're much like bait on this string. I tug on the string. She turns and crawls back towards me. I untie her, and she crawls up and around my arm, then crawls up my neck with the tenderness of innocence. I'm tickled by the beetle walking over my skin. Adventure takes her to the rounded cliff of my shoulder, back to the smooth valley of my neck, to the forest of my hair, and over the cavern of my ear. I block her path with my hand, preventing her from poking my eardrum with those twig-like legs. She crawls onto my hand. I hold the beetle up to my face, examining her eyes and the armor-like shell. Then I set the beetle down and let her roam free.

It's late afternoon and the heat outside the warm coolness of the den is unwelcoming. I hear the rev of wings and look over to her fluttering inches off the ground near my ear. She flies to the light of the exit and out into the open.

"Be free. Explore. Be careful," I tell her.

Remember me.

***

Within my normal radius of forage, I chop at an old rotting tree with what looks like termite holes spread throughout. *I haven't tried termite yet.* The wood is brittle and shatters off in chunks, revealing the worms that live in these holes. I've seen worms before. Eaten by my comrades. I came near to trying one myself.

> *"Try it," my comrade Hansuke said, while he held one in front of my face.*
>
> *I cringed.*
>
> *"Come on, it's not that bad," he tried to convince me. With the look on my face holding, he turned to Tetsu. "You?"*
>
> *"I'll try," Tetsu said, grabbing it from Hansuke's hand.*
>
> *Tetsu tilted his head back and dangled the worm over his mouth before lowering it down onto his tongue and chewing. Delaying his judgement while swallowing the bits of mangled worm, Tetsu turned to me. "He's right, it's not that bad."*

I continue chopping until enough of the worm is exposed to pinch one end of it. I pull out the long, stringy specimen embedded within the hole. It is indeed the same type that Hansuke offered me—flatter and slimier than earthworms, with one side like the whitish, secreting underbelly of a slug. I smell it and close my eyes. *It's not that bad*, I tell myself, thinking of Hansuke's and Tetsu's words to make the task easier. My experience with the *doku utsugi* berries and *hikagehego* taught me not to judge by appearance and is responsible for my botanophobia. Tilting my head back and dangling the worm over my mouth, I peek at it before lowering the worm and draping it over the surface of my tongue like Tetsu did. I close my mouth and chew, expecting my gag reflexes to kick in from the sliminess or a foul taste. The texture and taste are much like an oyster. I grind the worm down into small bits with my molars before swallowing. Chopping at the tree, I collect more. *Yeah, I always did like oysters*, I think as I pull them out of their holes. I'm not convinced by the rationale, but the taste, *it's not that bad.*

***

My emaciated face reflects from the pond. I have yet to find enough meat to sustain my muscle mass and wait for the macaques to return with insects providing just enough protein to prevent my muscle from altogether disappearing. My desire for meat is visceral. Grass continues to supplement my diet. "Air salad" is what I call it, because the grass is so light and tasteless that it barely registers as food when I eat it.

My attention turns to those canaries, as I call them. I have yet to figure out how to capture one. They are quick and unpredictable. I shift to their intrigue. *Unambitious or pragmatic?* It's the quick flaps of their tiny wings, the sharp whistles of their chirps, the whites around their eyes, and their nebulated markings that catch my attention. They are small and delicate. The meat would do little to satisfy me, with all the precision it would take to catch one. *Pragmatic.* I listen to them sing, and their colors become blooming tropical flowers blown from tree to tree. They are drawn to the large-old-tree that bears no fruit. The tree shades the den for a large part of the day, reduces the wind blowing towards the den during rainy season, and displays the canaries in close view from the den.

***

I trek further up the mountain, climbing around the steep rear-rock-wall and up along the soiled slope. I stand on a rock suited for a chair at the mountain's pinnacle and scan the landscape. *Hai. A grand sight.* Mountains stretch far northwards and southwards. *Overlook Point*, naming this viewpoint. In the transparency of thinning summer leaves, I locate the meandering line of a stream or rut along the side of the next mountain over. *More fresh water.*

After a half-day's walk down my mountain, southwards, and up the next mountain over, I arrive at a dried-up streambed. I follow it further up the mountainside until the steepness and disappearing rut halts my progress. I turn around and follow the line down the mountainside, closer to the abandoned village in the lower valley. Snap. I stop. I walk. Swoosh. I stop. I walk. *Who's there?* I kneel, looking towards the dark shape of a rotting tree trunk nearly my height, and prepare to catch the movement of another person. *Would I run? Should I say hi? Kumusta ka? Are they still looking for me?* I'm excited. I'm frightened.

Beyond the base of the mountain and near-centered in the valley is the dirt road that leads to the village south and to the unknown north, an overgrowth of grass and weeds hiding the potholes. Following the sounds of water trickling, water collects in the drainage gully along the side of the road from the combined nearly dried-out streams descending from surrounding mountains. The overflow of water from the obstructed flow in the gully, fans out across a washed-out section of the road. Much of the topsoil is washed away, revealing the hodgepodge of rocks beneath the clear, rippling water. Standing in the gully, I look north, gazing as far down the road as I can see. The road is suffocated by the encroaching jungle, both sides of foliage nearly joining at the middle with the tips of their reaching branches. I reach down to fill my canteen and drink, unabashed, as water runs down the sides of my face. Across the road is the continuing jungle leading to the adjacent mountain range. I look south towards the village where the road ends in the foothills soon after, while the other direction remains a mystery. *My way out?* as I look north. I hold my gaze, then turn my head back to the south. *Maybe the village is safe for me.* I return to the nook, knowing I've pushed boundaries far enough for one day. *Small victories.*

The village is bustling as I walk down the road out in the open, and people wave to me.

"Come on, Kaiyo," they shout out to me.

I wave back, elated at the sense of community.

"Ok. Thank you," I say, smiling as I enter the boundaries of the village.

Each villager smiles at me. "Welcome home, Kaiyo," they say as I walk past. "That way," they add, pointing to the village center.

I arrive at the village center. A hut sits in the middle of the open square.

"Your home," a man tells me.

"Thank you," I say, bowing to him.

"Go ahead. Make yourself at home," he tells me. The villagers gather around.

"It's all yours, Kaiyo," someone shouts.

"Welcome home, Kaiyo," someone else shouts.

A kid approaches wearing a skirt or shorts and coconut-patterned shirt. She or he points to the hut.

"Yoku nemuru, Uminom ng mabuti. *Eat well," the kid tells me, switching from Japanese to Tagalog to English.*

I enter the hut, and the villagers cheer me. A large bed with a soft mattress, a glass pitcher of lemonade, and a table covered with an assortment of food await me. I run towards the window to look out and thank everyone, but thick, cold, iron bars block me from sticking my head out.

When I look at the villagers, they no longer smile. I run over to the door, but more bars block my exit.

The man that led me to the house, now wearing a military uniform, stands on the other side.

"Make yourself comfortable," he tells me.

I wake and quick to exit the confines of the den.

***

On my return to Overlook Point, I note where the village is hidden and recognize that vague line at the bottom of the valley as the old dirt road. *What is to become of me?* I look north. *My escape? Tetsu, Hansuke?* I lie across the rock chair, the warmth from the stone heated from a full day of sun reaching me among the orange-purple glow of the evening sky. The instinct to decipher the landscape or plot my next destination is lost as I'm held above the valley by the chair's armrests, my head dangling.

The color of the sky changes to an orange-gray in the evening light. Silhouetted geese fly across the sky before darkness covers the valley and details of the landscape around me are lost. Moonlight reflects from the rock surfaces in a line of peaks, as if the mountain range was the glistening sharp points of a *tatsu's* tail.

Kami. I think of Shintoism's philosophy that all elements of nature possess a spirit.

"*Kami*," I mumble, looking at the rock I sit on.

"*Kami*," I say, looking at the peaks. "*Kami*," I shout, looking to the stars.

Is this my destiny? Why do I exist? It feels as if I'm the only one asking such questions. Or perhaps another soldier, from a different nation, hiding in a different jungle is asking the same thing. I'm bonded to this imagined soldier for only a moment before loneliness chills me to the core. My mind dies with me here when my body does. *Does it? Maybe the world will change. Or maybe I will change. Will I see Maeko, Tamiko, or Shiro again to explore such thoughts together? Oh my, how time was wasted.* I unwrap the banana leaf used to protect the Bible with the photo of Tamiko and Maeko between the pages. Their faces in the photo are the same faces imprinted in my mind.

"I hope you are well."

Maybe not all's lost. The approaching, hope-sopping rainy season threatens to extinguish what remains of that flickering flame. Holding the photo close to my chest, I fall asleep.

***

The blurring precipitation of heavy rain splashes onto the water-soaked ground, drenching my thoughts. The long wait begins for the sun to inspirit the jungle and my mind. As children, we enjoyed the rain.

> *Shiro and I were two years old when we first met, according to our mothers. I don't remember those early days, but I do know he's been in my memories since I began creating them. He's my brother—different mother, different father—but my brother. Shiro and I played in the rain, splashing through the sheath of water on the road with our bicycles, stomping through the puddles, and sometimes standing there idle as water ran down our faces onto our clothes.*

"Shiro, what happened to you, brother? Are you ok?" I say, looking north.

***

After months of rain, my joints strained much like my mind in huddled idleness, the rays of sun bloom life into the irrigated jungle. Using the momentum of nature's renewal, optimism sprouts within the soggy soil of my mind. The mosquitoes pester and nag. I use smoke from the fire to ward them off. They leave, return, pester. I rub a handful of mud onto my skin from a concave beyond the sandy soil, which has created a mud pit. Mosquitoes hover, searching and finding those spots of exposed skin unprotected by the mud. They prod at me. I leap into the mud for relief and roll around. I snort like a pig while slogging through the ditch and caking on layers. The mosquitoes hover near like a squadron of planes waiting for clearance to land.

***

Nature stirs all around me. *Kami.* The moisture sucked from the ground and into the air creates a hot sludge. *Why live another day? Meat? None to be found. Escape? All options end with death. Rescue? I'm forgotten.*

I struggle for action, sinking without motivation to stay afloat. *Useless.* All my titles stripped-clean and left to face my truth. *Truth,* I tell myself. *Only one truth.*

> *As a child, I questioned life and death. Those thoughts were not what a child should think of.*
>
> *"It's odd to think we will die one day," I said to Shiro.*
>
> *To no surprise, with young boys our age never thinking about the topic, he was quiet, probably giving it deep thought for the first time.*
>
> *Years later, I brought up the same topic. Shiro had a response. "Yeah," he said, "but isn't it odder that we are living now?"*
>
> *"What do you mean?" I asked.*
>
> *"If we die one day, why do we live today?"*
>
> *I could not answer him, and he did not expect an answer. But I thought about Shiro's question then and still think about it today. Why do we live only to die? Is it logical to*

conclude random chance of humanity, emotions, and the seemingly well-choreographed world around us? And if life is eternal, why do we experience this particular life, under the illusion it's finite, at all? What purpose does this created world serve?

Shiro and his family are Buddhist, Mahayana Buddhist, to be precise. Shiro would often talk to me about truth and reality.

"The Four Noble Truths," he said in our early teen years, "are about facing the reality of suffering in the world."

"What does that mean?" I asked.

"First, you must learn about dukkha," he told me.

I never did. But the idea of truth stuck with me.

Buddhists often speak of enlightenment. Maybe that's what they mean—the ability to know the truth of our raison d'être. Fear didn't reach me then and it doesn't now, but there's a hollowness within me. Unresolved issues with loved ones and my actions in war nag me while I contemplate the bigger picture and reason for existence.

I visit Joe.

"Hi Joe, let's talk," I say, as if we're sitting together drinking sake, and still caked with mud. "Where are you? Are you here or up there?" I ask, looking up to the sky. "Or are you everywhere, like *Kami*?"

I wait for a sign—a bird landing on my hand, a sudden change in weather, a face within the clouds, a voice whispering in the breeze, or a clear answer inserted into my thoughts.

Joe was born April 1915 on a corn farm in Nebraska to a large family of three brothers and three sisters. He was the middle child, along with his sister Margaret. Lost in the shuffle of a large family, Joe joined the army to get noticed. He was sent to the Philippines as part of the regiment tasked with protecting the country from us Japanese and looked forward to traveling to the tropics when told of the beautiful beaches and Filipinas.

He visited all the blue-water beaches and met a Filipina. They talked of marriage.

"You will love America," he told her.

"But I love my country. My family's here," she told Joe. "If you want to stay, we'll stay," he said.

While they were planning their marriage at the local municipal church, we attacked this otherwise peaceful country. Joe fled the village to ensure he wouldn't jeopardize the safety of his future wife and her family should we Japanese find out about their relationship. While in hiding, he joined the USAFFE to support the resistance, hoping to defeat us and reunite with his fiancée. He was separated from his fellow USAFFE soldiers in battle and fled further into the jungle to find safety. After weeks of little food and water, he rested at the front-cliff-wall of this nook, thinking it was a dead end. As his final act, Joe held the Bible close to his heart with the belief it would magnify the power of his prayer for the safety of his fiancée and her family.

This is how I envision Joe's story.

***

My charcoal-sketched calendar on the den wall turns to smears and blotches due to the wind, moisture, and my body brushing against the wall. *Time is running out. What's next? Action. Take control.* I splash water onto the wall and wipe it clean with a coconut husk. When the walls are dry, and with the blackened tip of a stick, I mark an x for the nook, draw a house for the village, draw two jagged lines on the top and bottom of the map to show both mountain ranges lining the valley, draw a straight line for the road centered between the mountain ranges, write "*Tenshi*" for the location of the Aetas' property and burial site, and write "Overlook Point" at the peak above the x. I find joy in the act of writing these few and simple words. When attending a poetry class in college, we would write a haiku and then use that haiku to write an American-style poem and vice-versa. I wish to do so now. I think of Matsuo Bashō and Emily Dickinson.

I need more names, more locations. Explore. Discover. Only the occasional gunshot remains, which could very well be hunters. I look to the black line on the wall drawn for the road heading north, which comes to an abrupt stop with nothing else ahead of it. *I'll explore that way. Prudence, patience,* I tell myself. *After the next rainy season is best.*

> *There, in the crowd of familiar faces, is the young Filipina girl from my dreams—short black hair, big eyes, and a constant smile on her face. It's a gathering at my childhood home on the farm. Food is served, among it, roasted pig. Shiro, Tetsu, and Hansuke are in conversation at one corner of the room. Captain Mori speaks with my father as they*

> *stand within the frame of the front door, each leaning their backs against opposite sides as if part of the frame. Shiro's parents and Tamiko's parents sit in the lounge. My mother is in conversation with Tamiko in the kitchen. Maeko and the Filipina girl, for whom I don't have a name, play coming in and out of the house, accompanied by laughter. This girl is part of this large group of family and friends, belonging there even though she is a stranger, her presence outshining everyone else as if in a world she created.*

I wake. The girl lingers in my mind for a few seconds, then disappears as I adjust to reality.

I stack all the coconut shells collected, pondering different ways to use them beyond the purpose of bowls, cups, and storage containers. *Chungcajon. How did the kids play this game? I must find something else to entertain me.* Creating games is not the answer when there's so much around me. *Explore.* The orange-purple evening sky illuminates the splatter of clouds in the foreground. I have yet to appreciate this common sight, even though I stare directly at it. I continue to stare until my heart catches up with what my eyes have already seen. *Kami.*

Years 3 to 5

The barrier has grown taller and grass is worn thin on pathways of tightly packed soil. Wearing only my loincloth, I carry my rifle, knife, knapsack, canteen, and the bolo with me for my first exploration along the road leading north away from the village. I walk on the roadside within the cover of the jungle. *But would anyone who sees me know I'm Japanese?* I continue north for about six miles and reach a sign that reads "Clark Air Base" with an arrow pointing. I go no further. I'm bound to run into Americans and Filipinos the closer I get to the base during that long walk to the province of Pampanga. The road that brought me hope is a dead end. Literally, death awaits me there. Shoulders drooping, I walk back south along the road.

Despite the overgrowth of grass and weeds on the road, I expect a military convoy to rumble past any minute, breaking through the young branches, flattening the grass and weeds, with one of their dogs barking at my presence as I try to hide among the trees. "A Jap!" someone will shout, the soldiers then saturating the hillside with gunshots. That's the easy way out, considering the alternative. *Yeah, quick death by gunshot*, I think, weighing my options as if I have a choice over my fate.

Back at the den, I draw one long line and write "Clark Air Base" at the end of it, then "Death End" in big letters, covering most of the blank space beyond. I sprawl out as if I just surrendered to those American soldiers at the airbase, knowing only the Aetas' property and the village remain as alternatives to the nook. But it's the Huks territory, as I've come to understand why the village was abandoned. *Huks in one direction and the Americans in the other direction. Should I continue to stravage and hope for the best?* My hands tremble, each possible action a gamble on my life. I spend all day sulking rather than pondering, with no plan or intention for action. If someone rattles the bushes of the barrier or if I hear the click of a rifle, I won't put up a fight. My world has shrunk back down to this small section of the jungle. Then I think, *This land isn't so foreign.* Japan has monkeys, palm leaves, coconut, heat, a rainy season like here. *Fear not. Be at home.*

***

Spring's numbered days of spirited growth begin. *Time to grow something.* I choose a plot where the ground is like the sandy soil of the den and churn it with the backside of the bolo. I stick the bottom ends of collected green leafy stems from recently eaten *kamote* and a few newly harvested ones into the line of ploughed soil. Their tops of green and purple leaves are exposed to the sun; I space the bunches enough so not to inhibit the growth of the neighboring bunch. I gauge the sunlight coming through the canopy of trees and begin chopping down branches to provide sunlight to the newly planted *kamotes*. The thumping carries far into the jungle, in contrast to the soft morning sounds. The pod of monkeys responds by screeching in the distance. I pause. The screeching stops. I chop again and the screeching starts again.

I once helped my father cut down a thirty-foot-tall white birch tree split in half by a typhoon when I was nine years old.

> *Shiro and I climbed to the top of opposite sides of the split tree.*
>
> *"I'm a bird, no, I am Samurai," I shouted.*
>
> *"I am Samurai," Shiro shouted, pounding his chest.*
>
> *The tree was a source of entertainment on the farm for the year before my father decided to cut it down. It was the first time I used a real axe and* gyokucho. *The use of these tools made up for the disappointment of destroying our playground. I grunted at each swing, focused on the base of the tree.*
>
> *"What's going on?" my mother shouted from the house, which was her way of saying she didn't approve.*
>
> *My father took over after my twelfth swing. One of his swings cut into it as much as my twelve swings did. When the two tree halves fell to the ground, the branches held them up just as the branches allowed a tumbleweed to roll along the desert sand seen in American Western cinema. We chopped the tree up, section by section, starting from the top of each half. By the end of it, I was as proficient with the axe and* gyokucho *as a nine-year-old could and shouldn't be.*
>
> *"Next time, you can do it all by yourself," my father told me.*
>
> *The wood fueled our irori for three years.*

***

My first crop, I think, when harvesting the *kamotes* around eight weeks later. I cut off the *kamote* tops and replant them. Soon I'll have more than I know what to do with. I sun-dry, roast, and mash the *kamotes.* My mother told me, "Too much of anything is not good" when I begged for more chocolate given to her by Aunt Hotaru. *Too much chocolate!* I can count on one finger the number of times I'd had chocolate by that age. The *kamotes* are fueling me, that I'll admit, but they're doing little to build muscle mass. *Meat. Pig. Deer. Rat! I'll take a rat. Anything!*

I prop up the small-rock-table from the den with a stick; a short string is attached to the bottom of the stick, and a dead beetle is tied to the other end of the string. I've seen this type of trap as a kid using *ninjin* as bait on the way up to Takao Peak.

> *On the way down, the nub-like tail and sprawled hind legs of a hare stuck out from under the collapsed stone. My first instinct was to lift the rock off the bunny, hoping it would pop up, shake off the debris, and follow me home. Once I accepted the hare was dead, I thought about taking the catch home and telling my parents, "Look what I caught," thinking it would bring praise my way, but I'm not a thief.*

Rabbit meat must be delicious. What else lives among me? That rustling in the leaves is constant. Using a cricket and chunk of coconut meat, I tie them on two separate strings to increase the odds of luring game with two tempting choices. I'll be satisfied with a collapsed trap and missing bait as proof that something does scurry around here. Nothing the first day, but I return the second day to watch a line of ants haul bits of the coconut over their heads like little men hauling marble stones out of a quarry. I re-bait the line with even more choices this time—beetles, *kamote* slices, crickets, and coconut meat. After multiple failed attempts, I disassemble the collapsing-rock trap and return the rock to my den. *Stay pragmatic*, I think.

***

The perennial rain and wind beat me into another season of remission and washing my stench away. I stay within the den stored with food and wood. Succulent raindrops pound like drumbeats and the tree-bending wind rumbles around me like a passing train. I forage in short spurts during pauses in weather and scurry back into hiding when the rain returns, much like a cockroach does when a light switches on. *How many more seasons of this until it breaks me?*

I wake to the slither of a snake. When I open my eyes and turn my head to the ground next to me, I'm eye to eye with a cobra. The snake, coaxed into the den by the flooded ground outside, pauses at my movement with his head rising in the air, evaluating whether I'm a threat with its eyes and sifting tongue. I stay still. The cobra's head drops, slithering towards the back of the den as if invited. I inch towards my bolo propped up near the entrance, my eyes looking back and locking onto the snake. When it reaches the back of the den, I leap for the bolo and quickly turn to face it. I'm crouched within the den and keep my back to the exit. The cobra bobs its head to my challenge, weaving it towards me through the air as its bottom half coils on the ground. There is no other escape route besides the bright exit of the den unless he squeezes out of the back corner holes where the water runs out between the rock slabs and rear-rock-wall.

"Banzai!" I shout, mustering up courage.

I stick the bolo out toward the snake to prod him for a reaction. The cobra lunges towards my arm, and his fangs clink against the metal blade, inches from my hand. I jerk my arm away. *Close call*, my heart racing. The near-miss of his bite injects me with adrenaline.

"Come on," I call out.

I keep the bolo raised in front of me as a target should the snake strike again. *Cornered. No escape. Will it charge at me?* I kick up sandy soil towards the cobra, trying to confuse it while giving myself time to plan my next move.

"Banzai!" I say again, as my emotion piques in a mixture of anger and fear.

I bait the cobra with the blade again, not extending as far towards the snake as before. This time, it strikes with head and teeth clanking harder against the metal blade. The collision against the blade disorients the cobra. I swing and strike it, cutting into its flesh below its head. The force of the dull blade knocks the cobra off balance. The cobra lowers its head onto the ground and tries to slither past me, pressed tight against the bottom edge of the den wall. I toss my knapsack over the snake at it exits the den and step on the covered cobra. While standing on the snake with one foot and uncovering his head with the other foot, I insert the blade tip, grinding it into the soil to completely remove the cobra's head, and flinging it away with the bolo.

"Ahhh!" I shout, displaying the snake to the sky. *Snakes beware.*

"For you, Maeko," I scream out. "See what your papa can do."

One of the few times I spent with Maeko alone was at the local cherry blossom festival when back from Manchuria. Maeko took a liking to a hand-crafted rag doll made from the fabric of old, worn-out clothing. Grabbing the doll from the table it was displayed on, she ran up to me.

"Please?" she said, her pupils reaching the top of her eyelids as she looked up to me, the gleaming sunlight rolling in her eyes with each slight movement of her head.

"How much?" I asked the woman selling them, although I knew I didn't have enough money on me.

"15 yen," the woman said.

"Please?" Maeko continued to look up at me.

I reached in my pocket and pulled out 5 yen. "Not today," I told the woman.

Maeko's face soured.

"Take it. Pay me later," the woman says, after seeing Maeko's disappointment and knowing me as a local.

I refused, grabbed the doll from Maeko's hand, and placed it back on the table. She held back tears and did not speak to me for the rest of the day.

***

Coming down from the nook to forage, the afternoon breeze whistles and rattles the leaves, blowing a smell of manure in my direction. I squint, sniff, and follow the scent to a pile of droppings. *It's not a pig*. Turning to the swoosh of a bush being plucked of its leaves, I spot the animal's dark-brown fur in the distance. I sneak closer. *Deer*. The rows of white spots on his back are much like the sika deer of Japan.

While traveling by caravan to visit my mother's childhood friend in Okayama, the sika deer ran along the hillside, hopping over rocks and bushes as if its legs were made of springs.

"Can I ride it?" I asked my mother.

"If you can catch one," my mother replied.

I'd peer out my bedroom window toward Mt. Gosasou whenever snow fell, hoping to catch sight of their brown specks against the white background.

It wasn't until a few years later, while attending grade school, and after I realized the humor in my mother's statement, that I saw another one. A group of deer wandered down from the mountain one morning, grazing on the grass fields of my school as Shiro and I walked to class.

I asked Shiro, "Do you think we can ride one?"

"How would you catch one?" he replied.

But if we did. If we caught one. Do you think we could ride it like a horse?"

"Why not? The big ones are strong enough. Maybe even the small ones," Shiro said.

I stood there staring at the herd, thinking how nice it would be to befriend one and ride it up to Takao Peak like a cowboy riding his horse, parting ways with him or her once at the peak, to be reunited for another adventure sometime.

I catch myself staring at the deer in disbelief of what's there before me. *What a beautiful animal,* I think, mesmerized by the patterns of his fur, blotched as if with a white paintbrush. *Focus.* I shimmy the lever on the rifle to break apart dirt and grime built up around the chamber. *Patience.* I raise the rifle, aim, and brace it against my shoulder. *Got you.* Boom! He stumbles to his knees, then falls over as the gunfire echoes. The deer kicks its legs, trying to stand. I run towards him while grabbing another bullet, struggling to load it from the shake of the run. With the rifle loaded, I approach the stumbling deer. His front two legs buckle each time he tries to stand. *Save the bullet,* I decide, lowering my rifle.

The deer rests on his side, breathing heavy in pain, gasping, eyes stretched wide open, and the soft filtered light of the sun reflecting off his pupils. I kneel next to him, life his head onto my thigh, and gently pet along his snout. I'm slow to rise and aim the rifle at the deer's temple. Bang! I'm nauseous.

I must have been less than five years old because I struggled to get my eyes over the windowsill even after climbing on top of the stool which stood against the wall under the window. I ran out of the house into the road, careless to oncoming traffic even though Shiro's parents seared into my mind to look both ways. I picked up the dove, which couldn't run away from me fast enough, as it flapped one wing, the other wing staying close to his or her body. I knew it was a dove when I picked him or her up because this type of bird was once used at the kabuki theatre when a princess wore little white doves for feet.

"They are doves," I heard a mom explain to her son in the row in front of me when the boy asked.

It was an odd sight, birds for feet.

"Are they real birds?" the boy continued.

The mother paused. "Well, yes," she said.

"Then why don't they fly away?"

I too wondered that while listening, believing the information was intended for all the curious kids that could hear

> *her.*
> *All the mother could think to say was, "Because they can't fly anymore."*
> *I waited for the boy to continue his questioning, but he was satisfied with his mother's answer.*
> *It was a special performance for mother and son that day, the room full. I was there with Shiro and his mother. Later, I learned the doves were taxidermied.*
> *"Dead and stuffed," my father said.*
> *The dove I rescued is similar to a pigeon but smaller, with a longer tail, and white just like the princess's feet, except alive. And I didn't want anyone to kill and stuff him. I wanted to fix his broken wing.*
> *I took care of Yuki for three years. I hid my crying from my parents when she or he died. This was my only ever pet. There was our family dog, Hachikō, who sometimes accompanied me on adventures, but his primary duty was to watch over the property.*

Already, taking the deer's life and not using the meat for sustenance feels like an injustice of equal proportion. I pay homage to the deer by putting my hands together and closing my eyes, much like in prayer. *Thank you for your sacrifice.*

"*Itadakimasu,*" I say before eating.

***

Drought has brought a scorched brown to the jungle. Smoke is in the air. *The Huks*, thinking back to the smoke in the air from the Aetas' burning house years ago. I follow the source and find a dried-out steppe with flames rolling over the yellow-brown grass and crawling up splitting, lifeless trees. I rush down to the field, its center blackened and flames lining the edges of the smoldering, charred ground encroaching the main treeline. *I must stop the fire, save the jungle.* I run to the burning field with bolo in hand and begin chopping at the ground as if to till the soil of an abandoned garden. Exhausted, I crouch over with hands on knees to catch my breath. A lush green thicket within the main treeline, with a shaded, oasis-like grouping of trees, much like the one in the nook, is across the way. *Pond?* I run over and burst through the thicket. *Water.* It is a shallow, muddy pond. I break off leaves and branches from the surrounding foliage, and dip them in the pond to collect water and mud. I sweep over a section of flames, leaving a trail of mud, before returning to the pond to repeat the process. The field smolders and I sit in the shade. My dire thirst gives me the will to fight through the exhaustion, get up, and make my way to back to the den to claim my canteen as if it were my trophy. *See what your papa can do, Maeko.*

It was a dry summer, Shiro and I were around seven years old. There was a grass trail, wide enough for a horse-pulled wagon, at the back end of the rice paddies which buffered the neighboring properties. We spent time there pulling each other on a cart with metal wheels, once used for hauling rice, that we salvaged from an abandoned lot. Along that trail was Mr. Nakajima's property. He was an old man, a farmer who lived alone after his wife died. We rested from pulling each other on the wagon in the shade of an old garage-like structure on Mr. Nakajima's property. Underneath the structure was thinning, dry grass. Shiro pulled out a small red box of matches from his pocket.

"Where did you get those?" I asked, excited to see them.

He grinned.

"Let me see," I said, holding out my hand.

He placed them in my hand. On the top of the box was a samurai fighting a tiger. I opened the box full of matches and pulled one out.

"What first?" I asked, and looked to Shiro.

I lit the match, walked past Shiro to the dry grass, and dropped the match onto the grass. The blades of grass were spaced far enough that the flame didn't reach the blades until it burned to its end. Ready to burn out, a single blade of dry grass touching the flame caught fire. I watched closely, urging the flame to grow. The flames travelled along the blade of grass as if it was a wick. The flame hopped to the another blade of grass and another. Momentum built, the fire spread. Grins of our amusement turned to the dumbfounded looks of what-do-we-do-now, when out of nowhere, Mr. Nakajima popped onto the scene in panic, grunting in effort while he stomped on the fire. Unable to stop the flames from spreading, he ran over to grab an old rotting piece of plywood which lay flat next to the shed, with moisture trapped between it and the ground. He threw the damp plywood on top of the flames. Shiro and I ran away while Mr. Nakajima smothered any red glow in the grass with the tip of his tatami sandals. We returned the next day, embarrassed of not only starting the fire, but also in failing to act. Our parents never acknowledged the news of our mischievousness, and the kindness Mr. Nakajima continued to show us after the event served as the perfect punishment, as it turned our embarrassment to shame.

The scorched earth of the steppe reminds me of that day, except shame is replaced by a sense of accomplishment. The smoke clearing from the air, I find a circle of rocks from a recent campfire sitting in the center of the field. I look around, my head much like the shifting head of the bayawak, then step back into the jungle. Taking an alternate, zigzagging route on the chance someone follows, I spot the symmetrical lines of a bamboo thicket among the trees and bushes. I brush away the dry leaves at the foot of fully-grown bamboo stalks to find young, sprouting bamboo culms and dig the soil around it with my hands before yanking the culm out of the ground. I harvest more of these bamboo culms and bring them back to the nook, and peel off the layer much like a corn husk until I get to the softer, fleshier, yellow-greenish center. I cut off the two ends, rinse any remaining dirt from the flesh, slice it into smaller pieces, boil them in a coconut cup, and eat the nutty-flavored, artichoke-textured vegetable. *Masarap.*

***

Midday and while out on a forage, I hear the caterwaul of macaques and run to the noise. As I approach, the long girth of a python stands out in the garnish of leaves and branches. It slithers downward, closing in on a confused young macaque who looks in every direction but behind as the other monkeys scream to warn her. The python snatches the young, unsuspecting monkey in his jaws. The snake's body coils around her like the large arms of a muscular man reaching around for a chokehold and cinching tight. She screams in a desperate call for help. The elder monkeys try to distract the snake from its victim by shooting in and reaching out as though to strike the snake. One monkey reaches far enough to slap the snake, to no effect, as the snake is already fully occupied by its catch.

Meat. I aim at the python without a clear shot and the risk of killing the young macaque. The captured monkey screams and I must shoot now to save her or put her out of misery. I aim at the snake's wide body, the macaque hidden in the coil. The python's head crests above the coils, only the arm of the macaque within his jaws. I adjust my aim. Bang! The snake's grip releases, and the monkey flails to the ground. *She's dead,* I think at first. The python drapes over the branch in balance of his two halves before sliding off and onto the ground next to the macaque. The macaque hops to her feet as if awoken from a short nap and shivers, frozen in place by the sight of the python next to her.

I step back to allow the other monkeys to help the young victim, but they continue to scream as they fixate on the dead python that lay there inches from the frightened young monkey. I walk up to and grab the tail of the python, dragging it away from her. She runs up a tree to a mother that waits. The pod screams and chatters in a different in tone. A mango drops from the tree. Gathering the snake and mango to bring back to the den, I look to the young monkey in her mother's arms. *You're safe now.*

The lean fat of cooked python meat still coating my taste buds, a tidal wave of dark, thick, towering clouds approaches. Thunder clashes like the strike of a *daiko* right above my head. The large tree stares at me with eyes from two old scars of chopped branches from when I first planted my *kamote* garden. The wind blows, swaying the creaking tree. The high-pitched chirps of birds warn of more to come. I motion my arms like a symphony conductor to the creak of the tree and chirp of birds. And with each creak or chirp, I point in the direction of the sound. I raise both arms to the *daiko*-like thunder as if in a crescendo, acknowledging the chiming leaves from a gust of wind. Then with a final bang of the *daiko*, my performance comes to a close in the fading reverberation. I bow to the rattle of leaves. Melodies from a *koto* play in my head. *Da da daaaa, de da, de da.*

***

At least three rainy seasons have passed since seeing or hearing anyone else. I trek down to the road where the weeds and grass are flattened or worn away by unknown travelers. Further down the road are fresh scars of chopped down trees. *Who do these people think they are?* The pestering mosquitoes return in small numbers, never again pestering like they once did, and the anguish of solitude weighs less on me. I hear the booms of yesterday's war as I fall asleep.

I wake to the young Filipina girl's face, but do not remember much of the dream itself. There were people around her, family, perhaps. In the lingering image of her, she's smiling as if that was the lasting image she chose to leave behind. She is not a stranger to me. *How would I know her so well?* Faces of many haunt me. Hers doesn't. It's a welcome vision. *A survivor perhaps?*

> *There was that village on the route to the prisoner camp in Capas along a major intersection with one road leading to Bataan and the other to the naval base at Subic Bay. There were kids, plenty of kids in the background. I remember each of their young faces that held a stoic naivety about what was going on. To look back on the sound of gunshots was to show concern toward the villagers.*

I did not look back then, but look back now, searching for this girl's familiar face. In the moment, my indirect participation or inaction seemed justified. *Nothing I could do,* was the common thought. A stain on my soul. I am comforted that the souls of thc innocent may exist in peace.

But those faces, of the children dead or alive, are vivid. I search for the girl somewhere there in the crowd that day. She is not there.

***

I've moved the firepit outside the den and fry crickets with coconut oil on a flat stone placed in the center. The pod of macaques plays nearby. The young macaque I saved last year approaches on the overreaching branch of the large tree and calls for attention. I grab one cricket, blow on it to cool it, walk underneath the branch, and reach up towards her. The monkey stretches out to snatch the cricket from my hand, holds it in her lips, resettles on the branch, and nibbles on it until gone. Her bulging eyes move back and forth between me and the frying crickets.

"You like?" I ask, grinning at her.

She stares at my mouth and tilts her head to the side from hearing my words, any words, for the first time. I grab another cricket and hold it short of her reach.

"You need a name. How about Kuriketto?" I ask, extending my hand closer to her.

She grabs the cricket from my hand. "Kuri?"

She chews. "Ketto?"

Her head tilts the other way.

"Ok, Ketto it is."

The pod calls. Ketto jets away with a sheepish squeak as if scolded for getting too close to me.

***

I retrieve the wrapped-up banana leaf, lodged between a gap where the two slabs of rock meet above, and unveil the dormant Bible within. Damage from moisture marks the leather cover and the edges of most pages, as if someone spilled tea on it. I open the center pages where the damp, bloated photo of Tamiko and Maeko sits.

"I'm doing ok," I report, as if Tamiko and Maeko can hear me.

I place the photo and Bible on the small-rock-table for them to dry in the air blowing into the den. Looking to the Bible, my thoughts turn to Curtis talking to me about Christianity. He explained how God is everywhere, and I told him it was like the *Kami*. Curtis often spoke of forgiveness, compassion, and love as essential to Christians, trying to persuade me to attend Bible study with him. I was worried about what people would think if I did, or if it was even allowed in Japan.

I couldn't understand the value he placed on the Bible and said to him, "It's just a book."

"It's much more than a book," he said, "it's the word of God."

I didn't understand how that could be possible, because what kind of God writes books? Still curious what the answer would be to that question, I step out and the sun punishes me for forgetting its power. Using a palm leaf to shield myself from the sun's rays, I visit Joe.

"Hi Joe," I say, as I tend to his gravesite by pulling the weeds that grow on top.

I sit.

"Things are getting better."

There's so much we could learn from each other.

I imagine what Joe's typical Sunday would have been back in America with his new family if he ever had the chance.

> *"Good morning, Joe," the pastor says, shaking hands as Joe walks into church with his Filipina wife and his two kids: a son named Ethan and daughter named Alyvia.*
> *They sit in the front pew, Bibles open while the rest of the congregation find their seats.*
> *The pastor tells stories of sin and forgiveness in everyday life, linking it to the day's Bible teaching.*
> *Following the sermon, the congregation gathers at the foyer. Coffee, tea, cookies, and what Americans call muffins are served.*
> *"I enjoyed the sermon," Joe would say to the pastor, and rehash some of the verses referenced and bring up related verses while flipping through his Bible.*
> *Joe's wife is in the background, speaking to another woman. Alyvia hops on and off the row of folding chairs lined up against the way as if performing gymnastics, smiling and saying hi to those who pass. Ethan sits calmly on a chair plucking on a string tied to a stick while speaking to the stranger next to him about his makeshift guitar.*

Should Joe really have a wife and kids, Sundays are absent of their father. The thought of that void in their life reminds me I still have a chance to fill the void in Tamiko's and Maeko's lives should they want me to.

I flip through the pages of the Bible. The first paragraph reads, "In the beginning, God created the heaven and the earth. And the earth was without form, and void; and darkness was upon the face of the deep. And the Spirit of God moved upon the face of the waters. And God said, Let there be light: and there was light. And God saw the light, that it was good: and God divided the light from the darkness." I read more each day, skipping through chapters and stopping on stories that catch my interest. Some of the stories remind me of *The Tale of Genji*, with kings replacing emperors. Curtis' words of forgiveness, compassion, and love resonate in my quest for enlightenment. I read on, turning away from the pure entertainment of some stories, and often referring back to already read or skipped pages. *Ah yes*, I think, as it dawns on me that Curtis never said God wrote the book. He said it was the word of God. As I gain a better understanding of the stories, I make sense of the sections titled with different names. *This Christian God is working or speaking through these people*, I think in revelation. I read; I study. My interpretation of the world is evolving, much like it did in college. Curtis' wise words on matters from science to religion did not fall on deaf ears. I merge this new knowledge with my abstract and altruistic spiritual perspective. Life in solitude, the spirit of all things learned from Shintoism and idea of truth in Buddhist philosophy, all playing a part. I understand the concept of God's Will in the Bible, which sparks my sense of purpose. Which God and what Will I attribute to this enlightenment, I have yet to determine. There is something more significant, more important than I. This I know.

α

Years 6 to 20

It is a dry summer after an unusually mild rainy season. The pod of monkeys encroaches on my den, playful and eager for me to feed them. I refuse, recognizing the dilemma I'm in. They start poking around the nook. An adult macaque steals a coconut shell full of cashews from the den. *This is bad.* I chase him. He spills half the cashews, avoiding my kicking leg and swinging arms.

"Shoo!" I shout, as I chase him away.

The other macaques swoop in and pick from the trail of nuts behind me. I chase them away.

"Ahhhh!" I scream.

As I become more aggressive, they do as well. The adults, at different positions around me, having already forgotten how I saved Ketto, taunt in their deep, brutish calls. I grab my rifle with its bayonet attached and point it at the monkeys. They flinch, then continue their taunts and rummage through my encampment.

"Leave!" I tell them. "Go!" I shout, as I run around chasing them away, swatting air with my open hand as I do with mosquitoes.

When I chase the macaques away on one side, a tide of them moves in on the other side. The surrounding circle of macaques closes in. The adult males take turns dart in at me. My heart races. Fumbling to raise my rifle, I shoot into the air. The monkeys scatter back into the jungle.

Days Later

I walk over to the monkeys' territory. *Just don't feed them,* I tell myself. The monkeys scatter and screech when they first see me. *Should I be doing this?* I sit on the ground with legs crossed. Their panic calms. After a few minutes, they ignore my presence. The young ones chase each other among the treetops and tussle on the ground. The adults guard the perimeter while grooming each other. Young monkeys approach me.

"Shoo," I say, careful not to shout.

They are skittish to my presence, which leaves that invisible boundary long held between human and wild animal intact. I shoo and throw pebbles to keep them at a distance without creating panic.

Weeks Later

I arrive this morning with the peering eyes of the alpha monkey on me. Before I'm able to set my things down, he climbs down, then leaps from the tree and charges at me. I hold my ground. He struts back towards the tree, then turns around and charges again.

"Hey, I don't want to replace you," I say with genuine belief that he understands my sentiment, as I step back, slouch, and raise my empty hands.

He charges at me as though my voice is a further agitation to him. *I have overstayed my welcome*. As I pack up my things, ready to abandon the companionship of the monkeys for good, he charges at me again with new confidence and set on seeing to it that I don't return. The inertia of his closeness reaches me. I keep him at a distance with my bayonet, striking the air in front of him so I can back out and escape. *Ok. Your territory*, I think, avoiding speaking for fear of causing further agitation. The alpha passes the sharp point of the bayonet, keen on taking a chunk out of my flesh, a crazed, rabid look on his face. He stretches his mouth wide open, shouting and flexing those sharp fangs while strings of saliva swing from his teeth. The other adult macaques begin to surround me and the window closes for a possible escape without injury. He is between me and the blade. With one hand gripping the barrel and the other near the butt of the rifle, I swing the butt forward just like I was trained. It strikes the alpha on the side of his head with a force that would crack a man's skull. He's stunned by the hit. *Attack*, I think, realizing this may be my only opportunity to make it out unscathed. Stepping back and flipping the rifle with the blade pointed at him, I thrust the bayonet through the monkey's right eye and into the back of his head. His body is quick to go limp as I pin his head to the ground while he convulses to his death. The pod of monkeys flees, screaming like villagers under siege of a massacre. The monkeys flee and I expect they will not return. *He was a father too*, I think, as I kneel next to the dead alpha, then bury his body at the base of a mango tree between the arms of its roots.

Soon after returning from Manchuria, Tamiko, Maeko, and I were at the market in Aki District searching for a happi *coat for Maeko. Much of the time, I walked behind them, focused on every movement and sound of the market. The piercing laughter of young children next to me and the boy squeezing his younger sister with a hug caught my attention. Their grins meant nothing to me as I watched to see whether he squeezed her too tight, looking at them, then to their mother standing behind a produce table of daikon, kabocha, and satsumaimo which the woman was selling. Tamiko reached over to the lady to purchase a handful of satsumaimo when a young man, working at the next stand over, handed a bill to the lady, asking for change. Tamiko pulled her hand back and waited. Maeko, next to Tamiko's side, stepped back out of the way to distance herself from the man's reaching arm. He looked at Maeko but did not smile. The young girl played with her brother next to me. She squealed. I flinched, catching the kids' attention. They looked up at me, and I relaxed my jaw in an attempt to smile. I turned back towards Maeko, expecting the man to acknowledge her or Tamiko.*

"Wait your turn," I told him, grimacing while looking dead into his eyes.

"Excuse me, sir?"

"My wife was waiting," I said, pointing to Tamiko.

"I'm sorry, sir," he said, expressionless and not looking to Tamiko.

"And you scared my daughter," raising my voice and pointing to Maeko. He said nothing.

"Are you going to apologize?" I asked, taking a step closer to him.

He faced me and stood tall, saying nothing. And as I lifted my left foot to take another step towards him, Tamiko grabbed my arm.

"Kaiyo," she said, squeezing my arm and looking up to me, "it's ok." Tamiko turned to the man. "He just came back

from Manchuria," she told him.

I broke eye contact with the man, surprised by her statement.

She knew before I did how much the war had changed me.

***

These patient trees, idle creatures, dominate in both size and numbers, working together. Each unique. Their pace of life is somewhere between the birds zipping around and the unmovable mountains existing for a millennia. My rhythm adjusted in adaptation to their environment. They wait, and although I can uproot and move, I feel less capable than them. It is as though these wise creatures are the true guardians of nature and of pure essence. The mountains tower above, funneling water into the valley, but do not see me. The sun covers Earth's surface, energizing life into these trees, but does not see me. The moon oversees the night, pulling and pushing the shorelines of our vast oceans, but does not see me. The trees see me, feel the vibrations of my steps, hear the rumble of my voice, and feed on the air of my breath. The melodies of my mother's *koto* play in my head.

I'm keen to climb the old tree, previously deterred by its maze of tangled branches. I run and leap onto the base, grabbing the lowest branch to pull myself up. I crouch on the branch, its bulk providing steady support. Looking upwards, I plot my path through the maze. Twisting and turning, I climb. The branches poke into my rib cage and claw at my neck while I shimmy my way up. I make it through the layer of twisted branches before facing another layer. Willing myself closer to the blue sky, I break through to the top. The stinging scratches on my skin are relieved by the cool, open air reaching me. I'm held up on the padded fullness of the jungle canopy as I indulge in the view, the same view as the birds and trees. This large tree shields and hugs my den below.

There would be the occasional glance my way by my father and my mother who worked, undeterred by weather or illness, somewhere within sight but always at a distance, on our respectable plot of land. As I grew older and stronger to help with chores, I received more attention from them as a laborer than a son. Observations of other children with their parents convinced me of this. A smile or look of affection towards them didn't reach my father's hardened heart or break through my mother's bubble of anxiety. As soon as I heard my mother tune the koto, *I would stop what I was doing and find a resting spot. If I was outside at the time, which I often was, I remained close so I could hear the calls of her tuning instrument. The distinctive sounds of off-note chords were like the gong of a bell at the temple. My curiosity of my home environment piqued Sunday night after putting myself to bed. I was drawn to the details of our home. It was my parents' only downtime. I lay staring at a candle's glow through the rice paper walls, watching the silhouettes. My father wrote his calligraphy while sitting on his tatami in the lounge, inspiring me to write in the air with my finger. My mother, with her normally deliberate movements, played in the next room as if she danced with the* koto, *swaying forward and back and side to side while sitting on her zabuton. I'd wait for the melodies to fill the air among the chirping crickets. Her elusive emotions came out in the music. I hoped that we as a family were somewhere in those melodies. I led myself to believe it was so, mimicking*

her notes with the hum of my voice. These were lullabies that eventually put me to sleep.
When my eyes drew away from the silhouettes and intricate veins of the rice paper walls to listen to the scratching of my father's pen and the boing of the koto's strings, I looked up to the weave of our bamboo roof. There, among the dark crevasses between the bamboo threads and wood beams, my eyes scanned for creatures that had found temporary refuge in the warm, dry comfort of our home: a spider hanging in its web vibrating from the draft of air coming through the gaps between our roof and the house frame, or a lone moth bouncing off the ceiling among the flickering candle light. I'd wait for the idle geckos to look my way.

***

Today, in year seven or eight, I return to observe the village. The property of one house in the village is cleared of shrubbery, ploughed, and fitted with the tan color of new bamboo window shutters. Staring down at the farm from the gradual slope and across the fields of tall *cogon* between me and the village, I wait for movement in the hut connected to that particular plot. The road coming into the village from the north splits the row of homes into two halves, each side equally balanced with an intermix of six bamboo huts and six small wood houses. The bamboo hut I watch is at this end of the village closest to me and where the road ends further south up into the foothills.

A young man exits, pumps water from his well, fills up a bucket, and pours the water over the lines of ploughed soil. *Eggplant, bok choy, sili,* I think, flipping through images in my head of those things I desire. *If it's rice he grows, he's doing it all wrong.* He paints all the lines of soil with water, then stands there looking over his garden. Scanning the garden from right to left, he then looks up, scanning from left to right over the grass fields, as if surveying the unused land. *Perfect for corn,* joining in his ambitions. Realizing his slow-moving gaze will soon set in my direction, I sink deeper into the cover of the jungle. I trek back to the den, my heart racing. *Excitement or paranoia?* I wonder.

***

The curtain of night closes on the jungle with sparkling specks emerging from the black canvas. The sidereal glow adds life to the otherwise dark void, each sparkle and streak with its own story. When my thought wanders away from awe at the night sky to introspection, another one streaks, as though to say, "Remember us?" It streaks then crashes to its death like a kamikaze. *I salute you. Nothing can endure forever. Love? God?* A day will come when these mountains around me, or the stars above me, will be no longer. A unique melody plays in my head. Tonight, the melody is further fueled by what gazing at the stars provokes. I believe answers to that one truth dwell somewhere beyond the realm of what we think is.

Not trained in music, I wonder if the melody is simply the reproduction of a song my mother played. The soothing sounds of my mother's *koto* are more vivid than many other childhood memories. I remember each melody without ever learning the names or stories behind the songs. I listened to her melodies as if her love was emanating from them. If given a second chance, I will tell her how much it meant to me, especially in contrast to the harsh words of my father.

Months Later

Corn stalks stand tall on a small plot in the once open field near the occupied hut, chickens cluck around the hut, and a firepit smolders not far from the well at the side of the home. As I walk across the field of waist-high *cogon*, there's movement in the house. I drop to one knee, the tall grass hiding me. The man exits and whistles. A dog emerges from the hut and jumps into the scooter's basket, with a few layers of burlap sack for padding. The man hops on the scooter and drives off. The dog balances himself in the basket amid the sway and rattle of the ride. The man drives through the village, heading south on the road that veers up to the foothills. Scanning over the village once again, I run over to the man's garden to pluck and peel back the green husk and silk. The bright-yellow cob inside gleams. *I do hope he understands.* Perusing through the other stalks, I pick two more ears, scanning the village and fields around me for any witness to my thievery as I do so. *But I'm not a thief.* The chickens cluck. *I'm not a thief.* I rush back into the treeline. *Did anyone see me?*

The man returns at dusk, untying and offloading a small burlap sack from the basket. He scoops rice out of the sack and into a pot, adds water, and the cast iron lid clangs as he puts it on the pot. He places a log into the firepit and carries the bag of rice into the house. *If I can get some of those rice kernels, I'll plant my own rice,* daydreaming more than plotting. Although I didn't bring extra water or food to last another day, I spend the night on the rounded surface of a large, moss-covered rock within the treeline, using ferns as a blanket. The glow of a lantern flickers inside the hut. Then darkness. We sleep.

It's morning when the man and dog emerge from the hut. If I had my own dog, I would also let him curl up next to me during the night. The man sweeps the dirt around his home into clean lines, pumps from the well, and waters his garden. I ready myself for him to jump up and say, "Someone took my corn!" He carries on tending to his property all day. Hungry and out of water and food, I do the long walk back to the nook before replenishing my body with corn and water.

Lying down for the night, I think of how to get some of the man's rice. I'm quick to wake in the morning. *Why don't I trade my* kamotes *for some rice? Or cashew, or coconut, or mangoes, or insects? Maybe not insects. Why must I plot, sneak, deceive? I will write a note and leave that behind, so not to expose my Japanese accent.*

Two Weeks Later

I return to village edge, predicting when the man at the house will run out of rice. I bring food, water, knife, bolo, all wrapped in my deer-skin blanket, my rifle slung over my shoulder, and my knapsack full of *kamotes*. After waiting three days, the man leaves with his basket. I walk up to his property and hang the knapsack of *kamotes* on a *balete* tree near the property's well—the note inside written with a charred piece of wood on a blank page from the Bible. I have only one chance to do it right and sacrificing one page of the Bible will be worth it if it works. Though I admit, I do feel guilty ripping out a page from Joe's Bible and God's book. The note, written in Tagalog, reads, "*Kamotes* for 1-kilo rice. Please hang here. Pick up tomorrow." I suspect he'll wait around for me, wishing to meet his mysterious neighbor. I will wait, spy on him, and retrieve the rice after he has fallen asleep. I should be able to retrieve the bag at night unnoticed. I question my spelling, because although I have learned Tagalog from the years interacting with the Filipinos before fleeing, I've read only a few words and never written the language. I do know that the use of "K" in place of the "C" is common.

I rest on the large rock within the treeline, anxious at the prospect of my effort for rice backfiring. *This could tip people off. That a stranger lurks.* "It's that Japanese soldier we never caught," someone would interject, and a mob comes looking for me.

> *I sneak up to the* balete *tree to pick up my rice. As I pull the knapsack off the tree, a box-like wooden cage drops down over me. I try squeezing through the gaps in the wood frame, try lifting it, and try chopping through with my bolo. I'm stuck, helpless. Villagers exit what I thought were abandoned homes and surround me.*
>
> *"We caught one," a woman says.*
>
> *"What should we do?" says another voice.*
>
> *"Kill him!" a man shouts.*
>
> *A boy steps forward and points at me. "Eat him!" he says.*

I wake in the middle of the night. The man's home is dark and quiet. My knapsack hangs. I creep up and grab the knapsack from the stub of an old cut branch. The man's dog barks from inside the hut. I hurry. The latch of the door clicks. I turn around, prepared to unsling the rifle from my shoulder.

"Po?" the man says.

Respond, stay silent, walk away, run. I flip through my options.

I walk, point to the knapsack, and say "salamat" as casually as I can, knowing that running is the act of a guilty man.

"Po," he shouts, now jogging towards me.

I stop and turn to face him within the moonlight, and a smile grows on my face.

"Salamat," I say again, pointing to the bag and preparing to walk away.

"Thank you for the *kamotes*. It's a lot. Thank you," he says in Tagalog.

I struggle to find words from the many years void of conversation, as though that dormant part of my brain needs warming up—much like an old engine. The unlatched door behind him swings open. I flinch at the dog running out towards me.

"Don't worry, he's a good dog," the man says.

My eyes fixate on the dog as he runs up to me and nuzzles his nose into my hand. My stomach sinks. *It's the Aetas' dog.* My heart races, a cold sweat forms over my body, and a willingness to kill percolates.

"He likes you," the man says.

Charge at him now. Choke the life out of him. Would that be justice?

I gather myself, breathe, kneel to pet the dog, and know that my rifle is slung over my shoulder should I need it. The adrenaline lights a fire under that dormant part of my brain. It's kickstarted to draw from a fragmented memory of social norms, and by the time words reach my mouth, they are a select choice.

"Where did you get the dog?" I ask with a smile, reverting to English and not worrying about my accent.

"A friend gave him to me," he says.

I continue to pet and look closely at the dog. *Maybe this man had nothing to do with the Aetas' death.*

"My friend had a dog just like him," I say, looking up.

His smile disappears. *Guilty.* He takes a step back, looking at my rifle. The revenge boiling in my blood reduces to a simmer when I see the fear in his face. And it makes sense why he's here alone, to escape the past much like me.

"It's ok, my friend," I tell him.

I retain a slight smile on my face, hoping it helps to keep him calm. I give the dog one last pat on the head and stand up. *Does the man know I'm the Japanese soldier, or just friends of the murdered Aetas?* Either way, he knows I know his violent past.

"Thank you," I say, raising the knapsack full of rice.

He reaches out to shake my hand. We shake, and I squeeze hard, holding it a few seconds too long.

Looking into his eyes, smiling the best I can, I ask, "How about chickens next time?" gauging whether I can trust him.

"Ok, *Po*," he says, nodding his head, his tight jaw releasing as he forces a smile.

I walk away towards the treeline and sense that the man continues to stare at me. I turn around. We make eye contact. He panics and runs towards the front of the property, where his scooter is parked on the main road. Kick-starting it, he revs the engine and drives off south down the road. This leaves him open, without cover of the hut and houses, unlike if he had gone north, shielded by the homes and more trees. I run across the field, trying to catch up to him, unsling the rifle, and aim. The dog runs after the man, confused over why he's been left behind. The man is in my sights, well-lit by the moonlight. *Clean shot.* I lower the rifle. *It's either him or me.* Sucking in air, I raise the rifle again with those few seconds creating more distance between us. I shoot. The man drops off the scooter as if he were a large burlap sack of rice. The scooter rolls ahead a few yards before tipping over and creating a dust cloud as it slides to a stop along the dirt road. The wheel spins. The man lies motionless. The dog runs up to his master, barking and whining. I run over to the man, the dog confused whether he should bark at me, lick the face of the owner, or run away. He does a little of all three, turning in a triangle of confusion. I carry the man's limp body to the hut and place him on the bed. His breathing is labored, eyelids are heavy, but his pupils peer directly at me as I kneel next to him.

"Why did you run?" I ask the man. "Things would have been fine."

His fear-glossed eyes pan over to me, and his lips separate as though he wishes to speak. The dog sits next to me. I tend to the man's wound, first pulling out the bullet from his back near his lung, sterilizing the wound with a bottle of gin from one of the many bottles on his table, then cutting strips of cloth from a white bedsheet and wrapping it tight around him.

"Stay with me, my friend," I tell him, so his mind doesn't give up before his body.

I remove the rice from my knapsack and cook it. Once he falls asleep, I sleep.

At first light, a motorcycle passing on the road wakes me. I glance over to look at the wounded man's chest to confirm it rises and falls. The passing motorcycle stops further down the road. *The scooter.* I peek out of the window. A pudgy, middle-aged man stands there, looking around for the driver of the crashed scooter, then glances back at the village. He gets on his motorcycle, turns around, and heads back to the village. I snatch my empty knapsack and loaded rifle before running out the back door. The dog follows me partway then returns to the hut and barks at the approaching man. The man watches as I sprint across the grass field.

"*Po*?" he shouts. "Are you ok?"

When I glance one last time, I see the man approach the house I fled from. I keep a brisk pace all the way back to the nook.

The fear-filled eyes of the injured Huk haunt me. A redeemed spirit. Despite his fear, it was as if he wanted to say sorry: sorry for killing the Aetas, sorry for killing the Japanese during the war, or sorry for running away and forcing me to shoot. *I just shot a man.*

I look at my rifle, hold it above me.

"If I didn't have this, I would never kill," I yell at the sky. "I'm a monster!"

I toss my rifle into the pond and the splash shatters my reflection. "Honor?" I scoff.

"Look at me!" I say, pointing to myself and to the jungle around me. "I'm in the middle of nowhere. No one cares. Where's the empire now?" I ask. "Damn the empire!"

I lie there, curled up, until falling asleep out in the open, the sunlight filtered by the large tree.

My guilt does not pass, sticking with me for days and accumulating on top of my other guilts. *I cannot use war as an excuse this time.* I fight these feelings and thoughts by numbing my emotions, which brings about lethargy. Starving my mind brings the same weakness as when my body was starved. I have no desire to eat or drink.

I'm in a foreign place, nothing familiar. Or is it fog I'm surrounded by? Not dark, not light. Shapes in the Grayness. Am I looking inward or outward? I pray. Lost with how to do so, I say, "Kami, Buddha, Christ," repeating it over and over while moving closer to a brightness.

I wake in the morning, mumbling these words. The melodic chirp of a bird reminds me of where I am. I'm familiar with many of the stories of the Bible in my accumulated reading, to the point I no longer read to learn but read for comfort. I recite in my head a memorized paragraph, *"But ask now the beasts, and they shall teach thee; and the fowls of the air, and they shall tell thee: Or speak to the earth, and it shall teach thee: and the fishes of the sea shall declare unto thee. Who knoweth not in all these that the hand of the LORD hath wrought this? In whose hand is the soul of every living thing, and the breath of all mankind."* This view of nature is a similar philosophy to Shintoism and Buddhism. I look to the jungle. *My dear Maeko, nature will speak to you in my absence.*

***

Anything beyond my need for survival is an indulgence. Focusing on food and shelter has weaned me off the old habits of society. I yearn for nothing except companionship. Thoughts of Tamiko and Shiro are strong, but do not grow stronger by the day, like thoughts of Maeko do. I know Tamiko and Shiro well and memories of them are clear. I'm getting to know Maeko in my thoughts, remembering my short time with her, imagining new moments, all accompanied by that melody. *Does she think of me? Does she forgive me?* I wonder while my fingertips caress the scar on my cheek under the fullness of my beard. *It's still there.* That day at the hospital vivid.

The smell of sake reached me first. I opened my eyes and Tamiko was framed within my vision like a well-composed Kajirō Yamamoto camera shot. She stared expressionless and left me confused about my predicament. I panned down to see Maeko's head sticking above the edge of the bed and noticed the white sheets and metal frame of a hospital bed. I looked around the room before reaching up to touch the stitched tightness on my cheek, and recalled the night before. I panned back to Tamiko, then Maeko. Their stoic stares magnified my shame.

***

The 10-plus years of heavy rains reshaping the contours of the valley exposes the flesh of hillsides, builds new hills of transferred earth, and carves new paths. The mound of Joe's grave blends into the slope, his remains at one with the soil. Using the bolo when necessary, I follow a natural trail and glide through the jungle in an easy stride, no longer creating a ruckus in my once-clumsy movements. My goal is to reach the peak on the other side of the valley. To keep from walking in circles when the sight of the peaks ahead and behind are hidden among the trees, I focus on a tree or large rock as a marker to move in a straight line across the valley. My sense of where the nook lies is never lost.

I cross the road, then a river, ending up on the other side of the valley. As I keep walking, the valley begins sloping up toward this destined peak. I look up to see the obscured shape of the mountain through the canopy of trees. Standing there at the mountain's base, I plan my route. I climb along a rut, unencumbered by foliage and making for an easy climb, until the slope steepens. My footing doesn't catch on the dry, loose soil of the rut, so I shift my path to within the softer, moister soil where trees and foliage grow. Once seen as obstacles to my climb, I now use the trees' firm base and the established roots of the foliage to hoist myself further up the slope while my feet sink into the softer soil for more footing. With legs pressing hard against the rich jungle soil and arms pulling on branches, I progress up the slope.

My neck stretches out the bulge of my Adam's apple while I look up to search for the peak. I catch sight of the peak above the towering rocky terrain leading up to it. My stance sways and knees weaken to vertigo. My fear of heights works in both directions, creating the sensation of free-falling upward towards the openness of sky as if top is now bottom. My hand trembles. Convincing myself of the reliability of gravity in preventing me from floating upward, I take a big breath and climb. Each step plunges into the sandy soil collected beneath the weathered rock and clear of any foliage. I press forward until reaching the angled rock wall which precedes the peak. Legs anchored, I thrust upward while my hands serve as the pulley on the jagged rocks. I progress up section by section in a near-vertical climb. Muscles burning, I will my way towards the peak. *I've come too far to turn around.* I press, I pull, I grunt my way up, then heave myself to the flat surface of the mountain's highest point on a protruding rock where the peak hangs over the conquered rocky terrain. Rising to my feet in exhausted glory, crouching over with hands on knees, I pant and gather my strength. I push off my knees and stand tall to gaze at the view. *This is all a miracle*, I think, in awe of my surroundings.

When my breathing finds a rhythm, I look over the ledge and down the rocky terrain to where sandy soil has already filled in my sunken footprints. *I did it.* While looking straight down with my feet gripping the edge carelessly, I sway in a playful taunt—the fear of falling down or floating up gone. Fear of exposure and the nook forgotten in the moment. *Look at your father now, Maeko.* Give me a parachute and I jump, give me a hot-air balloon and I'm happy to float higher. Then, once again, I think of the nook. From here, the rear-rock-wall marks the nook with a smudge of gray among the lush, green mountainside. *Home.* Looking away from the nook and at the landscape, I think, *this is my home.*

"Get back home soon," Tamiko told me as we lay in bed the night before I left for basic training.

"That will be my home for the next six months," I told her.

"Home is wherever your heart is," she said.

"What does that mean?"

"You may live in the army barracks, but your heart stays here with me."

I did not respond while I thought about that concept.

She slapped my arm. "I hope so."

"Of course," I told her. "I'm just thinking what's it going to be like. Will they let me think about you?"

"What do you mean?"

"Their goal is to make me a soldier first, and everything else is secondary."

"See! Why did you have to join?" she said.

"I'll be back before you know it. I'll walk out on them if I have to," I said, knowing it wouldn't be possible.

She knew that too, rolling to her side and placing her hand on my heart and me placing my hand over hers, only then regretting my decision to join the army.

Years 20 to 40

A new generation of bushes and small trees has joined our community, replacing the ones wizened or destroyed by the shifting landscape. A sense of belonging leads to thoughts of growing old in the den. Duty to myself and nature has replaced duty to my family with answers to my questions likely found in this carefully crafted environment. "Is this what happened to you, Joe?" looking over to his grave. "Did you give in, give up?" *I will always love you, Tamiko, Maeko.*

My pace, attitude, and appearance are more in tune with each passing day as I walk in rhythm to the swaying branches. My skin is darkened like the colors of the soil and tree bark, loincloth faded like the leaves and weathered rock, my hair hanging like the moss and vines. My breathing is gentle, like the constant breeze that soothes me from the heat. A place that should only be my temporary home is now a permanent home. All complexities of where, what, and how are simplified. *My home.* I no longer curse at the pounding rain or the nagging mosquitoes or the slithering snakes, as they are no longer antagonists to my well-being. The urge to shield myself from the rain, smack the mosquito against my skin, or chop the head off a snake is no more. The rhythm is in sync with the melody in my head. A single melody with crescendo and all. The sound is clear. I feel safe.

***

The village tripled in size since my last visit. Crops from corn to rice to sugarcane cover much of the modest slopes around the village. A new row of homes along a pathway perpendicular to the street encroaches on my viewpoint at the treeline. Garden patchworks of green, yellow, purple, and red vegetables are part of every home. Kids playing in the street part like water as a motorcycle drives through. Two men work in the rice fields. Produce stands made from salvaged wood line the streets, serving vehicles passing to and from the foothills.

The stir slows as the villagers filter into a white, concrete church with blue trimming in the spot where the community water pump once was. Only the two men working the rice field remain with their backs facing me. I walk further out and sit perched on a rock halfway between the village and treeline, listening to the sounds coming from within the church, with no commotion out on the streets except for the occasional passing vehicle.

"Oh Lord, Oh Lord, forgive me," I sing along with the congregation. The harmony and smoke of burning sugarcane provide a sweet incentive to relax. I place my knapsack on the rock where I sit halfway between the civilization and the jungle. The melody of song draws me closer with my dark skin, nappy hair, loincloth, and bolo on my waist.

An American military jeep drives north on the road coming down from the foothills. I sense the eyes of the soldiers on me as the jeep drives along the open road and approaches the village.

"Stop!" says a deep voice coming from the jeep.

The jeep stops. The passenger pulls out a pair of binoculars and peers at me through them. I walk towards the village as though I'm walking home, hiding my panic. There's mumbling, then the soldiers laugh.

"Yup, it's a negrito alright," he says, before gesturing for the driver to drive on.

As the jeep drives off, I look down at myself and touch my hair and glance at my sun-darkened skin to confirm my likeness to an Aeta before crawling into the grass on the slope leading down to the encroaching row of houses and near the garden of the first house. The tall grass gives me cover before I gather the courage to stand, hoping to blend in as a local or Aeta, anything but Japanese. I keep a casual stride with

shifting eyes as I approach the crops of the first house. I enter the boundaries of the garden with long lines of eggplant and okra. I look around, then reach down to pull okra off its stem.

"*Po*?" a young girl asks, hidden somewhere in the garden. Startled, I stand up straight and search for the girl, eyes scanning up, down, side to side.

"Can I help you, *Po*?" she asks, and I follow her voice.

She stands tall enough that the top of her head and eyes stick out above the next row of vegetables. I make my hand into a mouth as if I had a sock puppet, point to my own mouth, and shake my head to convince the girl I cannot speak.

"Tay," she calls to her father.

I breathe deep, my hand staying close to the handle of my bolo. The father looks out the window and casually walks over to us from his house.

"Can I help you, *Po*?" he asks.

I turn to the girl, urging her to answer for me.

"He cannot speak," the girl tells her father in Tagalog.

"You mean he's deaf ?" the father asks his daughter while looking to see if I understand.

I give the father a blank stare and raise my hands, pointing to my ears, then mouth, to convey both I can't hear and can't speak. The father looks over my thin frame.

"You want?" the father asks, pointing to the okra in my hand.

I nod, and the father looks to the girl. The girl runs over to grab a bag woven of thin strips of bamboo. The father and girl pick okra and eggplant, then place the vegetables in the bag.

"Go ahead," the father says as the girl hands the produce-filled bag to me.

I bow my head, thanking them, then look up to notice other villagers filing out of the church staring at me. *Did I just show them who I really am by bowing?*

In a panic to quickly break off from the interaction with the father and daughter, I say, "Salamat," immediately regretting it.

"You can talk," the father says.

I shake my head, pointing to my ears as though I can't hear, and the handle of the bamboo bag looped around the wrist of my other hand.

"I speak Ambala," the father says, which reduces my panic.

I shake my head again after he too has mistaken me for an Aeta. The father scans me from head to toe while the loud squeaking brakes of a passenger tricycle causes me to flinch toward my bolo. The father backs away.

"Go get help," the father tells the girl. The girl runs off. I back away.

"Help!" the girl shouts in Tagalog as she runs into the heart of the village where most of the villagers gather. "My father needs help."

The girl's shout echoes through the village. Other voices join in as the chatter of the village picks up. The father's and my eyes lock as I back away, then I move my hand away from the bolo after glancing to see that the man has no weapons. *I'm sorry, I'll go now*, reciting this in my head as an option to calm the tension. *But my accent. Better he thinks I'm Aeta.* The village commotion nears a fever pitch as the girl's and other women's voices are replaced by the rumbling of men's voices.

"Where is he?" an angry voice says.

I glance towards the village center and back at the father before running off. In the frantic getaway, I sprint back into the jungle without locating my knapsack. I look back towards the village to see a group of men approach the father. They talk, but knowing that they still don't know I'm a Japanese soldier, I must retrieve my gear so not to trigger a manhunt. I run back in the direction of the village and emerge from the jungle in plain sight to grab my knapsack from the rock.

"There," someone shouts, just as I snatch the knapsack and run off.

I dive into the jungle, the rumbling of men's deliberating voices behind me.

Back at the nook, the angry voices of men circle in my head. I view the photo of Tamiko and Maeko.

"Papa," I would like to hear Maeko say.

My father was once a soldier and always a drinker.

> *During my return from Manchuria and after putting Maeko to bed, Tamiko climbed into bed with me.*
>
> *Smelling the alcohol on my breath, she turned to me and said, "When are you going to stop your drinking and get to know your daughter?"*
>
> *"Drinking?" I answered. "I can't have a drink?"*
>
> *Tamiko rose from the bed, opened the drawer, and reached into the back of the drawer to pull out a sock with my sake hidden inside. She pulled the sake out of the sock and held it in front of me.*
>
> *"Why are you hiding this?"*
>
> *I scoff with a dismissive wave of the hand.*
>
> *"You put more effort into hiding your drinking than you do connecting with your family. How about your daughter?"*
>
> *"She's no good to me," I said while reaching for the sake. "Where's the son you promised me?"*
>
> *I stopped my words to the hiccup-like cries of Maeko in the next room. Tamiko got out of bed.*
>
> *"You've changed, Kaiyo. What happened to you in Manchuria?" she said, while walking out of the room.*
>
> *My emotional energy was locked in my own head, and I couldn't connect with Tamiko and Maeko beyond superficial interactions. It was like I was going through the motions of being a husband and father, minus the emotion. I*

thought of my parents and understood them better.

"Papa loves you, dear," Tamiko consoled Maeko in the next room.

"He doesn't love me," Maeko responded in her high-pitched voice of hurt.

I lay in bed and drank from the sake bottle until Tamiko returned to the room after Maeko had cried herself to sleep.

"You broke her heart," said Tamiko.

"I'm her father. Fathers don't care about crying," I said, slurring my speech.

"Did you drink more?" she asked, walking around the bed to find the empty sake bottle underneath. She picked up the bottle. "What's this?" she asked, then dropped the bottle on the bed next to me.

The bottle rolled down the concave of the mattress into me. I jumped out of bed.

"Don't throw bottles at me," I said.

"I didn't throw the bottle at you, Kaiyo," she said with a calm-guardedness as I took a clumsy but aggressive stance next to her.

Tamiko grabbed her pillow from the bed and walked away. "I'll sleep in Maeko's room," she said without looking at me.

"I'm sorry," I said, grabbing her arm.

Tamiko pushed my arm away.

"You're staying here," I demanded, grabbing her arm tighter.

"Let go," she tried pushing my arm away as I held tight. "You're hurting me."

She yanked her arm from my grip, ran to Maeko's room, and locked the door. I stumbled my way out of the room and into the hallway, then fell against the door to Maeko's room. My face rested against the door and my hand on the doorknob held me up.

"I'm sorry, Tamiko," my voice loud against the wood door.

"Tamiko?" I called out.

"Mommy," I heard Maeko say, waking up from her slumber. "Tamiko, please open the door," I said with a tired, slurred voice.

"What does he want?" Maeko asked.

"It's ok, Maeko. Your father is not well." I tapped on the door.

"Tamiko?"

I knocked on the door.

"Tamiko, I'm sorry. Open the door." I pounded on the door. "Tamiko!"

"Mommy, make him stop," said Maeko as her cries started again.

"Go to bed, Kaiyo. You're scaring your daughter."

"Open the damn door!" pounding harder on the door.

Maeko screamed above her cries.

"Stop it," she begged.

I went back to the bedroom, picked up the empty sake bottle from the bed, and returned to the door.

"Here's the damn bottle. Right back at you," I shouted as I threw and shattered the bottle against the door.

I fell to my knees, then laid my face and body on the ground next to the door.

"I'll just wait here for you," I said, eyes shuttering and passing out where I lay.

In the morning, I woke to the screams of Maeko. Tamiko stood over me. "Go back in your room Maeko." Tamiko pushed Maeko into her room and closed the door.

"Kaiyo," Tamiko said, kneeling next to me and touching my face.

I pushed myself up, Maeko crying loud on the other side of the door.

"Papa," Maeko called out.

It warmed me to hear her call me that for the first time.

"Stay there, Kaiyo," Tamiko said before running downstairs.

When I looked around me, there was a pool of blood. Soon after, I lost consciousness.

I came to in the hospital, with Tamiko and Maeko by my side and the tightness of stitches across my cheek. None of us found the right words to speak in the hospital room and on the taxi ride home. Maeko's eyes locked on to the scar on my face. When we arrived back at the house, Tamiko went straight to the kitchen and Maeko ran to her room. I packed my things.

Tamiko met me at the front door.

"Where are you going to stay?" she asked.

"The barracks."

"How long?" she asks, expressionless.

"A few days."

"Ok," she said.

I looked up the staircase and leaned over to shout, "Bye Maeko," softening my tone.

"It was too much for her. Give her time," Tamiko told me.

After three days, I delayed my return a week, then another week. During this time, America declared war on Japan after the attack on Pearl Harbor. I chose not to face Tamiko and Maeko again before going off to war. I did not drink again after that fateful night, but it didn't matter much because the damage was done, and I never saw Tamiko and Maeko again.

The scar across my cheek a dark reminder. I dream of Maeko uttering "Papa" to me one last time before I die.

***

It's been years since visiting the village. *How old am I now?* Time has picked up its pace here. The once long-lasting days are equivalent to three days now, what feels like a week is a month, experiences I thought happened over a period of one year is actually five. I keep a greater distance when I do return to the village and observe from a high ridge. More passenger tricycles travel the roads, but there's no sight of military vehicles. I hear the singing voice of a woman below. I step out from behind the tree and proceed down the ridge where a small waterfall flows into a pond. I climb down the slope, hiding behind the trees as I descend, until I'm close enough to get a good look at the singer. A woman bathes. She glances my way.

"Hey!" she says.

I straighten my stance.

"*Po*?" she asks, without scolding me for staring at her.

I hear the voices of more people approaching, break off our stare, run away closer to the village, and find a different observation spot. After assessing the changes to the village, I return the way I came and met by a group of men. I hold up my hands. *They finally captured me.*

"That's him," the woman steps up from behind the group. "Are you the pervert peeping at my naked wife?"

He waits for my answer.

I'm relieved they do not know I'm Japanese.

"Sorry," I say, while my eyes shift to the other men.

"They won't touch you unless I say so," the husband says while turning to look at the men.

"Sorry," I say again.

A man warming his fist in the palm of his other hand steps forward. I grab the bolo from my waist and toss it on the ground, not wanting to make this worse than it needs to be.

I'm beaten, thinking not to disappoint Maeko, until my face is bloodied, and ribs are sore. I wish no ill will on these men, despite the harm they are inflicting on me. I hope Maeko would see strength and not weakness. These are not bad men. I deserve it. I welcome it, despite the pain in my jaw and my swollen eye socket. Notions of violence have vacated my soul. I would only hurt or kill for the sake of loved ones, whether or not they love me back. Even then, violence would deepen my anguish, further tarnish my spirit. I came close to fighting for Tamiko before we were married.

> *I often let Tamiko drive my father's motorcycle-turned-tricycle while I rode in the passenger carriage. On the road we drove down frequently to get to the village center, a man emerged from his home, waving for us to stop. Tamiko pulled over.*

"A woman shouldn't be driving," the man said, as though it was his duty to enforce deviance away from our predominant social contract.

I knew her response would come before mine and would be better than what I could come up with, so I stayed silent.

"Why?" she asked.

"You should let your boyfriend drive," the man said, pointing to me.

"No thank you, I'd rather drive," she responded.

"Women don't drive," the man repeated.

I shuffled in the carriage and positioned myself to exit. It's about time I punched this guy in the face, I thought.

Tamiko revved the engine on the motorcycle and said, "This woman does," before speeding off and throwing me back in my seat.

Tamiko accelerated so fast that we nearly lost control and veered off the side of the road. I couldn't help to think, don't crash, please don't crash. Not that I was worried about injury to her or me, but that it would only prove the man's point. When I looked over to her, I saw the fierceness in her eyes on the road ahead and her firm grip on the handlebars. I knew we would be ok.

***

I gaze at the twinkling stars. My hand trembles. *Is life a test? A test of humankind, perhaps? And why does God remain obscure, an idea rather than something I can see, touch, hear? Or do I refuse to see a God that's in plain sight?* My questions echo among many others in the world, but in this setting, there's a purity in seeking truth. With another twinkle of a star, the notion of free will enters my mind.

"Ah, I see," mumbling to myself with eyes still gazing upwards.

Choice in a world I cannot control. Oh, how this makes sense to me. Choice, one of the few things I can control. I'm filled with a sense of control of not how I can change the past but how I choose to move forward. A light has been turned on in the dark corners of my mind, a contentment. Newfound hope sprouts from the despair of once only seeing dead ends to seeing the general direction in setting my life right. *The free will of choice. A gift. I'm an actor reading from a script otherwise.* I pray for answers. I pray for Tamiko's, Maeko's, Shiro's well-being.

But God? I continue to struggle with the idea of a god. *Which God? What constitutes God?* This well-crafted world cannot be possible from random chance. I look around at nature's stage that I've become so accustomed to, and reframe my perception. What I pray to in the sky, around me, or within myself, are one and the same. The soundtrack plays. I no longer fear strangers' eyes peering into this hidden nook with a sense my performance is viewed by acceptance by a singular source. The boundaries of familiarity expand out to the limits of my sight. The den wall is too small for my map, now written in my mind. I'm the overseer and not the overseen. I wish nature to flourish, to grow strong, fulfilling its roles. I often venture to ridges and attempt to peer out into a new set of unfamiliar landscapes, while staying within the hoary boundaries. My eyes are one set of lenses among many that tells one story within a much greater story.

I look far into the horizon and think of Japan, the beauty of the mountains and sea. I think of sushi, katsu, udon, miso. I miss the comfort of a kimono's silk against my skin. Most of all, I miss Maeko, Tamiko, Shiro, and my parents. The resentment I have for Japan is diluted by these positive thoughts, as I'm now able to separate wartime Japan from peacetime Japan. I burn the military patches saved from my ragged uniform and check to ensure the photo of Tamiko and Maeko is keeping well—now in the splitting leather sole of what used to be my boot, turned into a wallet.

Musical notes play louder in my head. The call of fatherhood beckons me like a faint radio signal, the prospect of returning to civilization more than hope. The trees, animals, and mountains speak to me, but there's no conversation; I can embrace them, but they cannot embrace me back; I am in good company, but lonely. I yearn to reunite with loved ones.

Years 40+

I sit on the slope looking down onto the now paved road that leads to the village in the south and Clark Air Base in the north. Power lines hang from their poles along the roadside with concrete block houses popping up within the jungle as if part of the spring growth. The sun glares off the tin roofs of those houses. The occasional automobile and motorcycle pass on the road. Approaching from the north and not yet in sight, the driver of a motorcycle, screaming down the street with an overworked motor, honks. I stand. A young man drives with a small boy riding on the back. They pass with the boy's arms hugging tight around the man to keep from falling and one side of the boy's face pressed against the man's back to shield himself from the turbulence of wind. Soon after, a rhythmic squeaking reaches my ears. I wait. My view is broken by the trees lining the road in the foreground of my sight. An elderly, shirtless man riding a bike comes in and out of view between the tree gaps.

He stops in open view in front of me. Mounted on his bike is a rifle, a bolo, a basket of *rambutans*, and two dead quails hanging from a metal rack of misaligned welds mounted above the rear tire. My eyes fixate on the *rambutans*. I salivate to thoughts of the mild sweetness and silky texture of their flesh. The old man props his bicycle against a tree and stands on the opposite side of the road, facing away, to urinate. Long, deep scars of bamboo lashes mark his back. I'm silent, still. Nature is silent, still. As the old man finishes relieving himself and turns around, I avoid looking at his face. The old man is slow to mount his bike. I wait for him to either look at me and nod or ride off without ever seeing me. He looks up and stares in my direction as the roar of a plane grows then shatters the silence when it flies directly overhead. The old man's eyes follow the plane. *Such a large plane.* My eyes fixate on the blue globe on the tail of the plane as it passes. *What nation?* I wonder. The monster plane leaves behind a soft vibrating hum as the old man hops on his bike and rides off. The squeaking reengages my ears, now sharper after the low roar and rumble of the plane, its rhythm returning to the same pace, as if the man is incapable of pedaling any faster or any slower.

***

I wake to a dog's crying yelps. The rush of fear clears the grogginess, and I follow the yelps down the front-cliff-wall to a medium-sized, golden-brown mutt stuck in a mud pit created by the recent rains. He looks up to me, legs deep in the mud, tail wagging, and whines. *I can't leave him there. He will draw the attention of someone.* I reach over to the dog with a branch. The dog clamps his jaws onto the branch, and I pull him onto the surface of the mud. When he tries to walk, his legs plunge back into the mud. I tug on the branch, his jaws gripping on it, and drag him along the surface of the mud while he lies on his belly. He now sits on dry soil at my feet looking up to me with a wagging tail.

"Smart, aren't you?"

The dog, made more excited by my voice, stands up.

"Sit," I tell him.

He sits back down. I reach over to pet him, and he lies down to expose his side. Then, as I rub along his rib cage, he turns onto his back, exposing his belly and brushing the dusty surface of the soil with his wagging tail. I rub his belly. He stretches his body by extending all four legs and closes his eyes in pleasure. When I stop petting him and stand up straight, he jumps to his feet, then sits back down, begging for more affection as he looks up to me. When I kneel to pet him again, he licks my face with his silky tongue. *His mouth is cleaner than mine.*

"Go home now," pointing in the direction of the village.

He glances that way but remains seated and stares back at me.

I lower my arm to reset and point again. "Go!"

He shifts and glances that way with his rear lifting off the ground for a second, before looking back at me and sitting down.

"Come on," as I lead him towards the village.

He follows.

We're on the outskirts of the village at the same place I used to sit and watch the Huk that I shot all those years ago. The dog sits at my feet, wagging his tail, and glances towards the village, expecting me to walk all the way with him. Homes fan out on both sides of the trails and roads, like the growing branches of a tree.

"Go," commanding him again, uneasy with my closeness to the stir in these homes.

The dog sits at my feet, wagging his tail.

"Go!" I shout, more firmly this time.

The dog runs out from the cover of trees, then turns towards me with its tail stiff and waits. He looks to the village and runs in circles, urging me to follow, but I stay hidden behind the treeline. He barks. I step back into the jungle. He barks longer and louder in excitement, running in bigger circles in the open grass field. I back into the jungle.

"Isko," a girl shouts.

I drop to my knees into the darkness of the shaded jungle. The girl, around six years old, runs out from her home about ninety yards away and into the grass field to the dog. She looks up in my direction and I sink lower behind the bushes.

"Isko, come here," she calls out.

Isko runs over to the girl, and she greets him. He licks her face.

"Why are you so muddy?" the girl asks Isko. "I've been looking for you."

A little boy, about two years old, runs out to join them. "*Kuya*, Isko is back," the girl says to her little brother.

Isko licks the boy's face. The boy turns away, cringing as he wipes off the saliva. The girl laughs and then runs back towards the home, which is a newer multi-room bamboo home on stilts, isolated at the end of a trail away from the main road. It is the closest home to my viewpoint. The little boy chases after his sister and Isko, stumbling as his short, uncoordinated legs catch on the grass in the middle of the field. Left alone, he hoists himself up and continues the chase.

"*Nay*," she calls.

The mother sticks her head out of the window.

"Look! Isko!" says the girl.

"Where was he?" asks the mother.

"I don't know, but he's muddy," the girl answers.

"Don't play with him until you wash him."

The girl runs away from Isko as he jumps on her in excitement. "Sit," she commands.

Isko sits.

"Tala, did you hear me?"

"Yes, Nay."

Tala pumps water from the well at the back of the home, filling up a bucket halfway. Isko sniffs the grass around Tala.

"Come here, Isko," she calls to him while lifting the bucket.

Isko approaches unsuspecting, his eyes and nose focused on finding a morsel in the dirt. Tala dumps the water over Isko, sending him running away under their home, where he shakes out the water from his fur. The boy laughs and claps.

The boy points. "Aso," he says, then laughs again.

"Jovin! Call him Isko, not *aso*," the girl, annoyed, tells her brother.

Jovin points. "*Aso*," he says again.

Tala and Jovin run, zigzagging in the backyard with Isko chasing them. The girl looks up towards me. I stand still, hoping to blend well-enough into the jungle. *Does she see me?* She returns to play. I sneak off.

***

I return to the village about once a month over the next year to observe the family—the trek wearing on the joints of my aged body. Today, I see Jovin but not Tala. I wait, scanning the area for her. Then I hear panting. Isko stands on the other side of a fallen tree near to me, staring, tongue drooping out, breathing heavy and tail wagging.

"Nice to see you again," I tell him while climbing over the fallen tree.

I greet him by scratching between his jaw and neck. Isko greets me by licking my outreaching hand. Snap! I whip my head up to the sound. Tala stands at a distance, watching. We lock eyes before she darts away out of the jungle. Isko abandons me to follow her into the open field and to the house.

A man at the property grabs her arm as she runs by, jolting her to a

stop.

"Why so fast?" the man asks.

I prepare myself to sprint back to the nook. "Nothing, Papa," she replies to her father.

The girl glances in my direction and I lean back to hide behind a

trec.

The father turns his head towards me.

"Did you see a ghost?" the father asks as he turns back to Tala.

The girl pauses then turns towards her father and answers with a firm, "No, Papa. Nothing."

The father lets go of Tala's arm. She runs into the house straight to the window that faces me and peeks out with her forehead and eyes showing above the windowsill. She finds me among the camouflage of trees. Cautious and shy, she waves to me. My first full smile since finding the nook reaches me, and I wave back.

***

Nearly a year later of continued visits overlooking the village and observing Tala's family, I venture further from the safety of the treeline, closer to the village. Tala and Jovin play in the grass field between the village and jungle. Tala occasionally glances over at me, Jovin unsuspecting of my presence while the mother prepares dinner, and the father is nowhere to be seen.

"Kick the ball," says Jovin.

Tala kicks the ball hard, and it flies over Jovin's head.

"Wow! What a kick!" he says, running to recover the ball.

Tala turns back towards me. I give her a thumbs-up and a smile. Tala grins from ear to ear, runs over to Jovin to grab the ball from his hands, runs back to her position, and kicks the ball again with that smile locked on her face, but not looking back up at me.

"Your turn, Jovin."

She places the ball on the ground in front of Jovin.

"Kick it."

Jovin kicks the ball, and it shoots sideways off his foot.

"Try again," she says, placing the ball in front of him.

Over and over, she encourages Jovin, until he finally kicks the ball over her head.

"Great job, Jovin!"

"Let me try again," he says with a grin.

I watch the kids for most of the day, then turn to observe the house where the Huk I shot once lived. A family appears. Like in Japan, these village properties are often kept in the family for generations.

***

A group of men gathered on Tala's property work around a large wood pole laid at the front of the house. I creep closer in concern over these strangers, until the men raise the pole with wires attached at the top. The hoisted wires sway from the pole, connecting to larger pole along the small side road. The men stabilize the wood pole in a pre-dug hole at the edge of Tala's property. One man approaches with a wheelbarrow, pours cement into the hole, and I cringe to metal scraping against metal as a second man cleans out the cement clinging to the bed of the wheelbarrow with a round-bladed shovel. The two men prop up the pole with recycled wood on four sides while the cement dries.

When the pole is steady, vertical, and the wires stop swaying, a man shouts out, "Ok."

Another man flips the switch box attached to the house and a hanging lightbulb within Tala's home turns on, doing little to illuminate the daylit interior.

"Electric!" Tala says in English, excited.

"Electric." Jovin joins in the excitement.

Their bobbing heads pop up above the windowsill while they dance in a circle around the light bulb as if doing a tribal dance around a bonfire.

"Electric, electric," they chant.

They continue to chant, and in clear view through the large window, the mother enters the room and pushes the button at the base where the lightbulb screws in, to turn off the light.

"Awwww," they say in disappointment, now standing on the far side of the lightbulb where I can see them.

The mother gives Tala a playful slap on her rear end as she walks away.

"It's electricity," she says to them in parting.

Tala and Jovin look at each other. "Electricity, electricity," as they continuing their chanting and dancing around the lightbulb without light.

***

Months later, voices come from the house. *Americans!* It sounds like they speak through a microphone. *Communications radio?* I flinch to the distorted sound of gunshots coming from the speakers. *Radio?* I move in closer, hiding within the *cogon* to enjoy the entertainment. In clear view through the window is the moving images of a small movie screen as I sit on the downward slope facing it. The mini movie screen sits on a cabinet against the wall across the room. The family's actions are framed by the window as they sit with their backs toward me. My sight is angled down from the slope, looking over the heads onto the screen. The father, mother, Jovin, and Tala sit together on a bamboo long chair with eyes fixed on the mini movie screen. I move in closer, farther down the slope, adjusting my angle until the top of the father's head is aligned with bottom of the screen. I'm away from the nook later than usual, as dusk brightens the screen and blends me into the darkness. A tired-faced cowboy with deep, throaty voice fills the screen. The light flickers in the home cinema.

"Bedtime," the mother says.

"Awww, *Nay*,“ the kids pout in unison.

The credits roll.

I cut and spread the tall *cogon* under and over me to keep warm. *I'll wake just before first light and return to the den,* I think, while listening to the bedtime chatter inside Tala's home.

***

Months later and consistent with my visits, I wait for days only to see Jovin and the mother enter and exit the house with glass bottles filled with water. I do not see Tala. On the third day of waiting, a man wearing a *Barong Tagalog* visits the home. Despite the full light of day, I move in close. The doctor pulls out his stethoscope, sits Tala up into view with her head drooping forward, inserts the earpieces of the stethoscope into his ears, then presses the diaphragm against her chest.

"Breathe," he tells her. He listens.

The doctor presses the diaphragm against her back.

"Breathe," he instructs, turning his head sideways to concentrate on listening while looking out the window.

He looks at me, then turns his head back towards Tala and places the diaphragm at a different position against her back.

"Deep breath," he tells her.

After the examination, the doctor steps out onto the front porch with the mother. He speaks to her, which sounds like whispers from my distance. The mother covers her mouth, holding back tears while Jovin kicks and pokes outside the home long-faced and disinterested in the things he kicks and pokes at.

***

I continue to observe the family every day during the week, feeding on insects and collecting spring water dripping through the crack of a fractured rock wall a short walk up the mountain slope. I wake this morning to chatter and find a group of people around the house, some crying. The mother is consoled by other women. The crowd quiets and turns towards the house. The father exits, eyes red, with Tala's limp body draped over his arms, and sits on the stairs of the front porch.

"Tala!" the mother cries out while resting her hand on Tala's forehead. Like a man is supposed to do, I hold my tears and flee into the jungle with the bushes whipping at me from the speed of my run. When I'm back in the nook, I stand on the sandy soil in front of the den and look up to the sky.

"She's just a little girl," I say, unable to hold back my tears.

I hop onto the large-stone-table. "What did she ever do?" I scream.

I lie flat on the rock as if to sacrifice my body to ancient gods on a stone altar. It is long and wide enough to support my body, except for my hands dangling to each side from my outstretched arms.

"I don't understand," I say, speaking softly to myself, "she never got the chance to live her life."

Raising my voice, "And me! I'm still here, alive, with all the terrible things I've done. Why?"

I sulk, grieve, cry, and scream, stretched out on that alter late into the night until I fall asleep.

***

"Bye, papa," Maeko says to me with Tala's face.

"Maeko," I cry out, half asleep.

It's morning. I fill my knapsack with all the collected cashews and some mangoes, loop the strap over me, then pick up the canteen, bolo, spectacles, and leather-boot-sole-wallet with photo of Tamiko and Maeko inside. I turn back to look at the den one last time and over the familiar surroundings of the nook.

"Thank you," looking up to the old tree and mountain peak.

I climb down the front-cliff-wall to Joe's grave and place the bolo and spectacle on top.

"Thank you, Joe. You helped to save me."

I salute.

Walking down the slope, wearing only my loincloth, I reach the

road. Motorcycles and automobiles pass me, with drivers and passengers giving me a quick glance. I reach the village and walk to that large rock out in the open close to Tala's home. I watch the people enter and exit the house to pay their respects, with very few people noticing my presence. I camp there for three days until Tala's body, in a white coffin, is taken from the house and carried by a group of men towards the church. Leaving all my gear next to the large rock, I lag far behind. I stand outside, near the entrance of the church, and listen to the priest speak.

"My God hath sent his angel, and hath shut the lions' mouths, that they have not hurt me: forasmuch as before him innocency was found in me; and also before thee, O king, have I done no hurt. Then was the king exceeding glad for him, and commanded that they should take Daniel up out of the den. So Daniel was taken up out of the den, and no manner of hurt was found upon him, because he believed in his God. And the king commanded, and they brought those men which had accused Daniel, and they cast them into the den of lions, them, their children, and their wives; and the lions had the mastery of them, and brake all their bones in pieces or ever they came at the bottom of the den. Then king Darius wrote unto all people, nations, and languages, that dwell in all the earth; Peace be multiplied unto you."

His words persuade me to enter the stone building with its large double wood doors. I stand along the back wall. People file past the open casket. The line grows and extends near to where I stand. One by one, people say their final goodbyes. I feel the moment slipping away from me as the line gets shorter. I'm last to get in line. People glance at me in my loincloth but carry on. When I arrive at the casket, I stare at Tala's face. *Is this the girl in my dreams?* I wonder as a similar familiarity hits me, a likeness. *Her eyes, her essence.*

I approach Jovin and his parents. They stand outside the church, acknowledging the parting mourners. Jovin uses his forearm to dry his red, moist eyes. His mother holds Jovin's other hand. I approach. Jovin looks up to me as the mother and father try to match my face to memory. They wait for me to speak.

"I'm sorry," I say to Jovin in English, with no effort to mask my accent. He rubs his eyes with the back of his hand. Feeling my words inadequate, I reach out, trying to console him. Jovin turns away. His father steps between us. A mixture of murmurs and questions come from the crowd.

"Who is he?" a lady says.

"Do we know you, *Po*?" the father asks.

"Capitan," a young boy calls out while running towards the scattered crowd walking to their homes.

"I'm sorry," I say to the father. "Tala," I add, putting my hand over my heart, "I'm sorry."

The barangay captain approaches with two other men by his side and the crowd steps aside to let them through.

The barangay captain walks up to the father.

"Do you know him?" he asks the father in Tagalog, turning to the mother as well.

"No, I don't think so," the father says.

The barangay captain turns to me.

"English," someone interjects with a gentle whisper.

"How do you know the family, *Po*?" he asks in English.

"I know Tala," I tell him.

"How do you know Tala?"

I look to Jovin and smile.

The barangay captain looks to the man next to him.

"He speaks Ambala," someone says, pointing to him. "Would that be better?"

"What's your name?" someone shouts.

"Do you know the family?" someone else shouts. "Where do you live?"

Overwhelmed and in panic, I try explaining in Japanese.

"He's Japanese," a boy shouts.

I turn to the boy. "I am Japanese," I say and with no more trembling in my hand.

***

I'm brought to city hall and provided a translator by a city official named Manny, with combed-flat, sleek black hair, and wearing a *Barong Tagalog* and black slacks. He gestures to me to sit. I sit, as he sits.

"How long have you been in the Philippines?" he asks, glancing over to the translator.

The translator's lips part, prepared to repeat the question in Japanese.

"I don't know," I say, bypassing the translator and answering in English. My eyes widen in curiosity to find out. "Since MacArthur returned," I tell him.

Manny directs the translator to sit, then talks directly to me. "MacArthur!" he shouts out with a smile. "You mean, since World War Two?" he asks in disbelief. "The war is over," he says, "did you know that, *Po*? It ended a long, long time ago."

The other employees rush into the office at my words.

"*Po*, please stay seated," a woman tells me.

She runs out of the office and comes back with a device and checks my blood pressure. Then she checks my pulse and flashes a small light onto my pupil while a man sets a cup of water in front of me.

Turning to Manny, the nurse, or at least I thought, nods.

As she exits Manny's office, Manny says, "Thank you, doctor."

I glance back at the woman as she walks out the door. *Woman doctor?* I can't help thinking. Manny is quick to continue our discussion.

"Japan surrendered soon after MacArthur returned and America executed devestating attack on Japan," he tells me.

I stare at him, waiting for more information. He stares back in hesitation, as if worried the steady stream of revelations will overwhelm me.

"It's 1990," he says, lowering his tone, eyes squinting as if sorry he must break the news.

I gasp, wide-eyed.

"1990," I say with a smirk, looking at Manny in disbelief.

It's a dream, that's what this is.

Manny smiles once recognizing my amusement. The room is silent as I digest the news. Manny and the translator give me time to do so. *When will I wake up?*

"We'll contact the Japanese embassy and see if we can find your family," Manny continues, breaking the long stretch of silence.

I nod, still gathering my senses after the shock. "Wife?"

I nod. "Children?"

I nod. "Daughter," I say, with my mind struggling in a daze to comprehend the time warp I find myself in.

I provide Manny with my personal information and pull out the photo of Tamiko and Maeko.

"That's my daughter," pointing to Maeko in the photo and smiling at Manny and the translator.

I try handing Manny the photo. "You can find her?" I ask.

"We'll try," he tells me, "but you keep the photo for now. Ok?"

"Thank you, sir," I tell him, bowing and nodding in gratitude.

We shake hands, and as the translator accompanies me out of the office, Manny says, "Tala's family has agreed to host you. Jovin explained everything to his parents."

I look at Manny, expressionless, as my mind churns.

"Apparently, Tala and Jovin often spoke with each other about you."

"Too soon," I say, feeling I'm intruding so soon after her death.

"They insist," he says. "Tala's mother thinks it will help Jovin. And you saved their dog, didn't you?" he asks, provoking another dumbfounded smirk on my face.

When I exit Manny's office, the mother and father greet me outside, Jovin hanging on to his mother's leg.

"Hi, Kaiyo *Po*, I'm Erwin," the father says, reaching out his hand.

We shake hands, and within his firm grip, I find comfort.

"This is my wife, Maricel," he says, pointing to her.

"*Po*," says Maricel with a smile, Jovin idled up close to her.

"And you know Jovin," he says, looking down to Jovin.

Jovin squirms in shyness, then smiles.

When I arrive at their house, the scent of vinegar and soy sauce of newly cooked food fills the space. The combined room of lounge and kitchen is adorned with all bamboo furniture. A table sits in the center and that lightbulb that Tala and Jovin once danced around hangs above it. Curtains drape the entrance of three bedrooms. A dark-brown caribou carved in wood, standing out among an assortment of other figurines, is displayed on the shelf against one wall. The mini movie screen sits on a cabinet, with a long bamboo chair in front of it, on the opposite side of the room. Above the mini movie screen is a painting of a hut next to a lake at sunset with a silhouette of a man pushing a banca with a long stick, green lakeside grass and treetops, yellow setting sun, and orange sky. Although I've never seen the painting before, it's nostalgic. After I'm done perusing my new surroundings, Maricel leads me to a room by brushing aside the curtain.

"This is Tala's old room. I hope that's ok for you?" Maricel says.

"Yes," I respond, shaking my head to approve this even though I'm uneasy about occupying Tala's room.

The small bed which Tala used has been replaced with a large bamboo bed, and the room has been cleared of all her personal belongings. *Too much.* For them to wipe away her presence from the room on my behalf places pressure on me not to disappoint. There's a folded stack of used clothes on the bed. *Too much.* Resting on top of the stack of clothes is a soap bar, towel, razor, toothbrush, toothpaste, and black plastic comb. I set my knapsack and canteen on the floor next to the bed and the leather-boot-sole-wallet with the photo inside on a small side table. *I must bathe.* Picking up the soap bar, towel, razor, and toothbrush, I exit the room. Erwin, Maricel, and Jovin turn to look in unison.

"Eat first," Maricel tells me as she carries a pot from the kitchen countertop and places it on the already-set table. "Eat now," she tells me again.

Is it ruder for me to refuse or ruder for me to sit unbathed and in my loincloth? I'm starving!

"He probably wants a bath as much as he wants food," Erwin tells her.

It's the latter.

"I will bathe," I say, showing the soap, towel, razor, and toothbrush. "Please eat," I tell them, "Don't wait for me."

After I exit the house, I hear Maricel say, "He must be starving though."

You are right, Maricel.

I pump water from the well into the bathing bucket, dump water over my head and body using a small plastic cup, and lather myself with soap. The luring scent of vinegar and soy sauce speeds up the process. I rinse off and wrap the towel around my waist before removing my loincloth, washing it, and then finish cleaning myself. I use rusted scissors hanging by a wire on the well pump and cut my hair before shaving my face as the last step. I put on a pair of jeans, white T-shirt, socks, and pair of light, soft, and well-padded white shoes with dark-blue symbols, which look almost like a checkmark, on the side. I re-enter the home with the family sitting at the table waiting for me.

"A new man," Erwin says, the whole family smiling in pleasure at my new appearance, which reduces my embarrassment that they all waited for me.

"Please sit," Erwin tells me, gesturing to the chair across the table.

I sit and Maricel stands to serve me from the pot of reheated pork adobo in front of me.

"Eat," she insists, "don't be shy."

Shy! I just don't want to be rude by following my desire to stuff food in my mouth.

It's the salty, tangy flavor of vinegar and soy sauce that explodes my taste buds. I could drink the juice from the adobo. Instead, I pour much of it over my rice.

"Masarap," I tell Maricel.

"Thank you," she responds.

I continue to eat, conscious to keep an appearance of patience and fighting to keep myself from crossing that line to sloppiness.

"No, thank you," I say, glancing up to her. "Salamat," I reiterate.

A moment of sloppiness is displayed while slurping up the adobo juice and the rice with soft strands of sliced onions mixed into it.

Jovin giggles. I look up to see everyone smiling.

"You eat like Isko," says Jovin. "Jovin!" Maricel scolds him.

"We understand, Kaiyo *Po*," says Erwin, putting me at ease.

Not forcing me into conversation, Erwin talks about Tala and the rest of his family. Erwin's time away from the family is because he's in the military, causing me to shift in my seat when I hear this.

"A good girl," he keeps saying.

Tala and Jovin are the closest thing to family here, and by default, Erwin and Maricel are too.

"I'm sorry about Tala," I finally say, interjecting with sincerity. The room silent, I look to Erwin.

"You're a good father," I tell him.

Then I look to Maricel. "You're a good mother."

Maricel's eyes water up, but she withholds any tears as she looks over to Jovin. I smile at Jovin. He smiles back.

"She was a good girl," I say spirited, trying to bring closure to our emotional frailness.

We finish dinner, speak in light conversation about Tala, the family, the village, and I speak a little about the nook where I lived all those years.

"Where did you sleep?" Jovin asks.

"In a cave," I tell him. "I made friends with monkeys and fought with monkeys," I say, leaving Jovin to ponder that in his imagination.

I thank them again before going back to Tala's bedroom while Maricel smiles from the other side of the room, still hiding her sadness from Jovin. But later that night, when Jovin is fast asleep, I hear the sniffles of her crying. The Bible says there are angels around us, reminding us we are loved and that we possess the gift to love. Tala rescued me. She gave me a path out. She is my angel.

***

With my strength regaining from a healthy diet, a good bed to sleep on, forming relationships with Tala's family, and the town as much a part of nature as nature is part of it, strength of mind, body, and soul builds. The void of lost loved ones weighs me down. I remain isolated from the other villagers. *Do they despise me? Do some of them seek revenge?*

I'm called back to the municipal building for another meeting with Manny.

"We could not find your family members, *Po*," he tells me.

I pull out the photo of Tamiko and Maeko, which I always carry in a real leather wallet given to me by Erwin, and hand it to Manny.

"You take this now, it may help," I say. Manny looks at the photo.

"Your daughter is much older now, *Po*," he says, pointing out a reality about her appearance I never considered.

"My wife is the same. Older and more gray but the same," I explain.

He takes a deep breath.

"Hiroshima, that's where you're from, right?"

"Yes," I answer.

He explains how the Americans dropped atomic bombs on Hiroshima and Nagasaki, describing it as "the biggest bomb ever used in war."

"Only one bomb," I say, not conceiving the magnitude of it, "maybe it missed them."

"It was a big bomb, Kaiyo, very big bomb," he explains.

I lean forward, close my eyes, and hide my face in my hands, remaining silent for about a minute. *They are gone forever.*

"Sorry Kaiyo, but you keep the hope. You never know."

Visions of the blast, the screams, haunt me in the darkness before I remove my hands from my face.

"Good news," he finally says, trying to cheer me up, "the embassy has found your enlistment records and confirms your citizenship. They are willing to fly you back to Japan."

I don't respond.

"You do want to go back, don't you?"

I look at him, hoping there's no need to explain what I'm feeling. The years of hoping to one day reunite with Tamiko and Maeko are extinguished in one moment, just like the lives of my wife and daughter. *If Tamiko and Maeko are gone, why would I leave my only family?*

I look out the window in his office in the direction of my new home.

"Do you want to stay here? We can arrange that if you want."

I nod at Manny.

"Ok, we'll sort that out for you, but we'll continue to seek out your family. Everyone needs family," he says to me.

***

That evening, after Maricel and Jovin are asleep, Erwin and I sit and talk under a *mangosteen* tree. Clouds are silhouettes among the background of the moon and stars. Erwin drinks a small bottle of gin with a label on it of a yellow-winged angel, wearing a red outfit and holding a sword over his head ready to strike a fallen angel. The artwork reminds me of a Michelangelo painting.

"Do you know much about the bomb?" I ask Erwin.

"The atomic bomb?" he asks, confirming with me before continuing with, "It was the biggest bomb ever used. Killed hundreds of thousands of people."

"Why so many?"

"Science," he says, before turning to me to say, "Sorry about your wife and daughter, Kaiyo *Po*. Apparently, the Americans thought that an invasion would cost too many lives."

"So many innocent people though," I say, in my first display of anger since emerging from the jungle. "Maybe an American invasion would have resulted in more innocent lives lost," regaining my rationale. "What do you think?"

"I think it sets a bad precedent," he tells me. "Anyone, any nation can find justification, any excuse for using the bomb. And now that all the powerful nations have the bomb, there will be no winners. We all lose. You're a soldier too, what do you think about it, *Po*?" he asks me.

"War becomes all about winning. Rules of engagement, morality, humanity, are all lost in war." I look Erwin in the eyes. "I hope you never see war, Erwin," I tell him in the docile nature of my fragile, elderly state humbled by war.

A recurring nightmare of Tamiko standing and burning up in the street visits me again and again, each time her scream making me nauseous, helpless, jolting me awake in a cold sweat, the sting of an imagined burn on my own skin.

***

The community pitches in to build my very own *nipa* hut on a vacant lot next to Tala's family. *How can these villagers forgive me?* In return, I volunteer to help manage the terraced rice paddies separating the village from the jungle's treeline where I once stood observing Tala and Jovin at play. At times, I retreat to my hut when overwhelmed by the interaction with the villagers. *It will take time.* It is at night, among the sounds of crickets and sight of bats flying across the moonlit sky, that the marooned soldier in me returns on occasions when I cannot assign a source to what I hear, see, or smell. I do not sleep until resolved.

Late morning, a woman approaches along the raised trail separating the rice paddies as I plant rice in the water-soaked field. She is at least ten years younger than me.

"Kaiyo?" she calls out when I dip my head to refocus on my work. I look up.

"Are you Kaiyo?" she asks in Japanese.

My mind takes a few seconds to catch up after spending years of speaking English and Tagalog.

I assent by raising my eyelids and nodding. She bows to me, and I bow back.

"I'm Atsuko from Japan International Newspaper," she tells me.

I find myself staring at her smile, then continue the motion of planting rice while I listen.

Atsuko goes on to explain she's enthralled by my story.

"Over fifty years!" she exclaims.

Do I want this woman to pry into my life?

"I will help you find your family," she says, convincing me in her optimism.

"You think?" I ask, questioning her rationale.

"Do you have any other family not living in Hiroshima at the time that may still be alive?" she asks.

"No," I'm quick to say. "My wife, my daughter, my parents all lived in Hiroshima."

"Ok, I'll focus on your wife and daughter."

"Shiro!" I call out.

"Your brother?" she tries clarifying.

"Yes. My best friend Shiro," I say.

"Did he live in Hiroshima?"

"Right there, the house behind me," I tell her.

"Ok," she says, looking down at her feet.

"But he was away during wartime," I clarify.

"Give me his full name and I'll look for him too."

She knows, like I do, both are ominous outcomes, but by the apocalyptic nature of the atomic bomb, it seems that the prospect of Shiro surviving is greater if he was not in Hiroshima at the time and away in battle. Atsuko notes all the names on a small paper pad and makes the promise again of finding them or finding out what happened to them before she leaves, making sure I understand that it's likely they didn't survive.

"I want to know what happened to them," I tell her to show that I accept the grim outlook.

We exchange bows.

"Why do you wish to help?" I ask, questioning her motives before she walks away. "Is it because you want to write my story?"

"I'm not doing it solely as a reporter," she assures me. "I think I can help."

I trust her.

***

This once village is now a town with a population of a few thousand. Some of the elders who were alive during the war are not so open to accepting me. Manny, the former unofficial mayor, is the official mayor of the town, now that the community is big enough to need a fully-functioning government. The town thrives because it's the main access point to the mountain range where there's a military training base, logging, mining, outdoorsmen, and tourists. The road into the foothills now extends over the mountain range. The town is also a place the Aetas come down from the mountains to access the health clinic and school. I've asked about the Aeta man and woman who saved me, but no one knows about them or the incident those many years ago. I did find out the man and former Huk I shot survived, only to die years later from tuberculosis.

"Maganda umaga, *Lolo*," Jovin and the neighbor kids would say each morning.

Apo Paling is Manny's mother. She is the most respected elder in town and at least ten years my senior. She sits on the porch of Manny's white brick house.

"Kumusta ka, *Po*," I say as I approach, intimidated by her cold stare.

Her eyes follow me to the gate of the property as she looks down on me from the high perch of the porch along the recently paved street.

"Kumusta ka," I say again, standing at the edge of the porch and bowing in return to my Japanese traditions.

She raises her chin in acknowledgement, refusing to exchange pleasantries.

Her stare chilling, I continue to speak in Tagalog. "Can we talk?" I ask.

She waves me up to the porch. I open a black metal gate customized with a fanciness of curves and whirls fitted on top, enter the empty carport, and walk up the driveway. She turns her head towards me once I enter the enclave of a porch made up of palace-like white marble and white tiles. I grab her hand and touch the back of her hand to my forehead in blessing, as is the custom here with elders, before sitting next to her. We both face the street while she flaps a bamboo-woven fan over her face with the other hand.

"Your husband fought in the war?" I am direct in the question, as she does not have the patience for small talk with me.

"Yes."

Silence.

"He died in the war," she continues.

"I'm sure he died bravely," I say.

She scoffs. "That doesn't matter. Never able to raise his kids. Over there, an empty grave," she adds, pointing to the town's graveyard at the end of the village.

Although her response is confrontational, I couldn't agree more, but stick to my agenda and avoid dissecting the topic. I don't think she would take my perspective as a former Japanese soldier all that seriously.

"Your son, he's done well for himself, the family."

"My son? I'm sure he would rather have his father."

Should I even bother with this?

With no intent to challenge that logic, I say, "I'm sorry," then look to her for a reaction.

Her face and posture do not change, as she continues to fan herself and not look at me.

"Only when I started reading the Bible did my guilt begin to go away," I tell her.

Head tilted down and eyes looking up at me like a schoolteacher gazing up at unruly students from her classroom desk, she puts her finger in my face and says, "Christ," then returns to that same cold look.

I wait for more, never taking my eyes off her. She turns her head away, then back towards me, in a quick glance.

"Ok," she says, with a nod.

Although the Bible has helped with my spiritual journey, she believes I've become a Christian. And it's not that the Bible hasn't convinced me of the sacrifice of the man Jesus, it is that I also find truth within the values and philosophies of Shintoism and Buddhism. They all create the patchwork of my spiritual self.

***

Erwin, now with higher rank, visits the American military base on Subic Bay near Olongapo City every three months for what the soldiers refer to as *Balikatan* meetings between American and Filipino soldiers. It is about a three-hour drive from town. I'm allowed into the civilian corridor of shops, bars, restaurants, and the beach within the official boundaries of the base. I'm amazed by all the advancements in technology witnessed best in this complex: the Japanese automobile, military jets, and the computers found in wide use at banks and business offices. I stop in place and stare in awe at the jetliners each time they pass. *Someday I will fly.*

> *"You know the calculator?" Jovin asked when trying to explain the computer to me.*
> *"Do you mean a mathematician?"*
> *Jovin laughed and took a deep breath, his eyes shifting in thought.*
> *"Ok, Po. Do you know what an abacus is?"*
> *"Of course. It's known as a soroban in Japan. The ancient way of calculating."*
> *"But instead of moving beads up and down, imagine a device doing it for you and all you have to do is type the equation and it gives you the answer."*
> *"That's a calculator?"*

"That's a calculator and computer. The difference is a calculator is only numbers. A computer is numbers and letters."

"But you don't need to calculate letters and words," I responded.

"In this case, you do. The computer uses numbers and calculations to produce words. It's one big, very complex abacus."

"But how does it produce words with numbers?"

"I couldn't tell you exactly how, just that it does," said Jovin, ending the conversation.

I pondered the thought and reached the conclusion a combination of numbers represents a letter in the alphabet, much like devising a secret code or number key to communicate military secrets to avoid enemy detection.

My Japaneseness is not an issue with this new generation of soldiers. In fact, Japan is a close ally with the Americans now. *Who would have thought!* I accompany Erwin on the bumpy ride in his custom-made silver sheet metal jeep. As usual, we part ways after he parks, with a 3 p.m. meeting time back at the jeep.

I'm always keen to strike up conversation with Americans, preferably with the civilians because it is hard to completely relieve myself of the ingrained guardedness to people in military uniform. I find the Americans friendly and a way to improve my English, because much of the conversations with the Filipinos now default to Tagalog or, at the very least, a mix of English and Tagalog called Taglish.

Today, it's an American man who sits on a bench along the walkway and faces the palm tree covered, sandy, resort-like beach. He eats lunch out of his green-colored metal lunchbox with its polished-silver latch, his black-and-white dog next to him. I join them on the bench. Th

American tells me he's a welder who builds and repairs military ships at the shipyard, and the Labrador's name is Rocky. I reach down to pet Rocky, who sits near our feet between us. Rocky wags his tail but stays seated next to the American.

"He looks like a good dog," I say, attentive to Rocky.

"You want him?" the American says, splitting concentration between me and his ham and sauerkraut sandwich, with mustard and mayo seeping out from the edges of white bread.

"Excuse me?" I ask, looking to the American with suspicion.

"I'm leaving for the States in a few weeks. If you want him, you can have him."

Caught off guard by the American's nonchalant attitude towards the dog and impromptu offer to a stranger, it takes me time to find a response.

"He looks like a good dog and our dog Isko did die recently. Don't you want to take him with you?" I ask.

"Yeah, he's a good rascal, but my wife and I are having our first child soon. So, if you want him, he's yours."

"Now?"

"How about you come back next week, same time, and if you're here then he's yours. If not, I'll find someone else who'll take him."

I ponder the thought on the ride home to town and during the week. It would be another commitment further rooting me to the Philippines, when I still have hope that either Tamiko, Maeko, or Shiro will draw me back to my homeland. Maricel, Erwin, and Jovin are like family, but the reality is they're not. The love we have for each other doesn't have a limit, but a sense of incompleteness in me persists. And since moving into my own hut, I try to keep a healthy distance, careful not to further infringe on their lives.

A week later, I see the American snapping the latch on his lunchbox with Rocky at his feet as I walk towards them.

"Ah, there he goes," the American says as he stands.

He unhooks Rocky's leash from the bench, eager to get back to work.

"He's a great dog but I just couldn't convince my wife he would be ok around the baby."

The American kneels on one knee and gives Rocky a firm rub under his neck with both hands.

"You take care of..." the American looks up to me.

"Kaiyo," I say.

"You take care of Kaiyo."

The American stands, then grabs his lunchbox from the bench. "He's officially yours," he declares, handing me the leash.

"Thank you," I say, as the American takes one last look at Rocky.

"A girl or boy?" I ask.

The American looks to Rocky, then back at me. "Ah the baby," the American's face brightens. "It's a girl," he answers. "We've named her Karen."

"Good," I say. "Very good."

"Do you have kids?" he asks.

"A daughter. Maeko," I say, forcing a smile despite the fact I'll likely never see her again.

***

Three years of sparse communication with the newspaper reporter, Atsuko, pass as she continues to seek answers about the fate of Tamiko, Maeko, or Shiro, while I've given up all hope. She writes:

Dear Kaiyo, I hope you are well. I continue to search all public records for your family but did not find any information on your wife or daughter. As you know, you have very few close relatives since your mother had one sister with no kids and your father did not have any siblings. I located records of distant relatives far removed from your family tree and will pursue this lead further if you wish for me to do so. Please let me know what you decide. Also, I did find the military records of Shiro. I regret to inform you he was stationed at Iwo Jima during the February 1945 American offensive which was soon after General MacArthur retook the Philippines. I do hope this bad news doesn't discourage you from finding out the true fate of Tamiko and Maeko. I will take some time off from work with the recent passing of my mother to tend to the funeral and her affairs before returning to the office. However, since I'll be in Hiroshima prefecture, I will visit the main archival building for the area when there. Apologies for any delays in receiving my next letter. Sincerely, Atsuko

***

Dear Atsuko, My condolences to you and your family for the loss of your mother. You do not need to apologize for any delays. It is very kind of you to visit the archival building while you grieve your mother's death. Please take all the time you need. Thank you very much and for all you have done already. I did not know you are from Hiroshima prefecture, maybe we are related. Hearing Shiro died at the battle for Iwo Jima leaves another void in my heart. Rumors about the battle on that island trouble me, and I hope he did not suffer much. He was like a brother to me. I will visit the church to honor him, since there are no temples here. As for these distant relatives, Tamiko's and Shiro's families are more family than these strangers who carry some of the same blood as me. Please do not waste your time and energy seeking them out. Be well. Sincerely, Kaiyo

***

Dear Kaiyo, Sorry for my late reply. Grieving and tending to my mother's affairs took a larger toll on me than I thought and have decided to resign from my position at the newspaper. I now reside in my mother's old home in Hiroshima. I continue my commitment to finding out what happened to your wife and daughter and now have more time to do so. I found records of Tamiko's and Maeko's last place of residence before the devastation of Hiroshima. However, when I visited the house, it had been rebuilt into a shopping center. I'm not sure if it was destroyed in the war or as a result of urban growth. I doubled my efforts to find Tamiko's and Shiro's families after your last letter when you said they are more like family than your distant relatives. I can confirm that Tamiko's parents survived the war but died of natural causes later in life. Unfortunately, much like your parents, Shiro's parents were victims of the bomb. My next move is to follow the lead using the last known address of Tamiko and Maeko. In regard to being related, aren't we all. Sincerely, Atsuko

***

While at the local market, I look for music CDs of the *koto* or other Japanese music. Lasers, is how Jovin described them.

"It shoots lasers, *Lolo*," he said to me.

He sees me as his real *Lolo*. I just wonder if he understands we are not related. He's twelve years old now. As for shooting lasers, I thought it was his imagination at work, but come to find out, he's not that far off. With a few CDs of Japanese music in my hand, I find a CD with a Japanese woman holding a *shakuhachi*. *A woman playing the* shakuhachi*?* I buy the CD because her eyes look like Tamiko's, along with two other CDs with Japanese singers of modern, westernized music. Pop music is what they call it. I will judge after I listen. Borrowing a radio with built-in CD player from Erwin, I listen to all my new music. The two pop singers entertain me. I'm moved by the music of the *shakuhachi* musician, listening to the entire CD again and again.

***

Dear Atsuko, I'm sorry to hear of your troubles, and please don't worry yourself with my affairs. I will rely on the Japanese Embassy to locate Tamiko and Maeko if they are still alive. Please take it easy and I will follow up to see how you are doing. Thank you for all you have done. Sincerely, Kaiyo

***

Dear Kaiyo, Please allow me to finish what I've started. I made a promise to you and intend to keep it. You will get no more help from the embassy unless the information falls on their lap. Although yours is an exceptional case, consider the number of people they deal with daily. Besides, I have nothing else to do with my time right now except this and my writing. I have no plans of working again anytime soon. I will return to Hiroshima archives to see if Tamiko's or Maeko's name comes up in any other documents dated after the war, which will help determine if they survived the bombing even if it doesn't tell us where they live. Sincerely, Atsuko

***

Dear Atsuko, I can't express my gratitude enough for your dedication to finding my family. The only thing I can think to offer is the CD I included which contains some music that may help soothe your soul. It caught my eye because the performer reminds me of my wife. How times have changed, a woman playing the *shakuhachi*. Sincerely, Kaiyo

***

Years later, Erwin is promoted and stationed at military headquarters in Manila. Jovin is the one who tells me.

"*Lolo*," he says with the brashness of an emerging teenager, "we're moving to Manila," he announces, failing to look at me with bottled up emotions. "Tay is moving up in the world," he goes on.

"Aren't you excited?" I ask him, to provide some optimism. "Big city, girls, lots of girls." If anything would get a fifteen-year-old excited, it should be girls. *Or is he still too young for that?*

"But all my friends are here," he says with a frown.

I hope he's sad about leaving me as much as I am to see him go.

"And you, *Lolo*, what are you going to do here alone?" he asks, finally looking over to me.

I smile at his words, and he's right. He checks on me almost every day.

"Lolo?" he always asks, sticking his head through the window or doorway, "Are you ok?" with a more admirable sense of concern over my well-being than he has for my privacy.

"I have Rocky," I tell him.

But in this moment, he downplays his concern by shrugging it off as if he's not dependent on me as much as I am on him. Erwin and Maricel welcome a busy lifestyle, as they will forever mourn the loss of Tala. There are few things to keep me busy in my old age except my mind dwelling on the memories of Maeko, Tamiko, Shiro, and Tala. Jovin receives much of my affection, with little opportunity to allocate to anyone else.

"It will be ok, Jovin," I tell him, "I will visit you often."

His frown levels off. I know this is not true and I think he does too, but my words seem to put him at ease.

***

A new family rents the old house of Erwin, Maricel, and Jovin. It is a young family: wife, husband, and their three young kids. Besides the pleasantries when frequently crossing paths, the man and I had only one real conversation. He introduced himself as Arnel and works as a tricycle driver. That is the extent I know them, as they seem comfortable keeping it that way. I do not think less of them for it.

I receive a modest income from selling fruit and vegetables on the side of the road. I'm too old and weak to work in the rice fields anymore. The years marooned in the jungle have sped up my ageing process and my body is in decline. The doctor tells me it's my kidneys that suffered most.

"Malaria, diet, the water could have done it," he said.

"Can you fix it?" I ask, thinking with all the advancement since World War Two that this longtime health issue of repairing bad kidneys is resolved.

"Avoid stress," he tells me.

I'm disappointed that he doesn't propose anything else.

Since coming out from the jungle, any stress rolls off me like a raindrop, as I now understand what I value most. *I am at peace here.* Only the suffering of strangers and loved ones before death, and regrets of never sharing the love I have for Maeko weighs on me.

***

It's been nearly a year since I heard from Atsuko, and I believe she's finally given up, despite her promise. It doesn't bother me because I never expected any good news, or for her to keep at it this long, often telling myself *no news is better than bad news*. I exit the hut early Sunday morning, clean-shaven and wearing black slacks and a *Barong Tagalog* sized and made just for me, which I wear every Sunday. I gaze at the morning landscape while I wait for Sunday mass, the soft light of the rising sun showing the lifting fog over the rice paddies. Attending church is the norm around here, and it's just as much social as it is spiritual for me. Just as when I turned to the Bible when marooned, I approach the sermons with a curious mind.

I stroll out to the paved road like I often do on a quiet Sunday morning. A woman stands on the road. She stares at me. I stare at her. Then I notice the glistening of tears on her cheeks in the dim morning light. I walk out onto the road, the balance of my thin, frail legs tested among the rocks that line the edges of the road. I step into the center of the road and regain my balance on the sturdiness of the smooth pavement. I move towards the woman, my eyes moist with the familiarity of the woman's face without yet sorting who she is. *I know her,* is all I think. Someone from my past. A tricycle comes down the road, then honks lightly at the woman. She does not move. The driver slows to a stop and the passenger steps out.

"*Po*?" the passenger asks the woman who's dressed in black slacks and a white button-up shirt.

"Are you ok?" the driver joins in.

The familiar woman's attention is locked on me.

The stir on the normally quiet Sunday morning street catches the attention of my neighbors. One by one, they emerge from their homes, seeing the woman and I standing in the center of the road.

"Kaiyo *Po*?" the young neighbor girl, Ruby, asks in concern.

I reach out to this familiar woman and pick up my pace in the long walk towards her. *I know her.*

"Papa?" I read the mumble of her lips.

"Maeko?" I ask, my voice trembling from old age and emotion.

"Papa?" she calls out, louder.

The dull look on her face now a sour frown of pent-up, painful emotion. "My daughter!" I say, turning to the villagers along the way. Villagers idle up to road's edge with smiles, their hands extended in support with gentle brushes from the tips of fingers as I pass. Maeko walks towards me faster than I can towards her. Staring as we get closer, then coming face to face, we both look deep into each other's eyes in final confirmation that the other person is who we think they are. It is easier for me to remember her eyes, the eyes of her mother, the unique essence of Maeko. *How does she know? She was so young when I left her.* But my eyes are the only part of me she could draw on which remains the same from her childhood, all else a dramatic transformation since then. My appearance old and worn, my soul loving and free as it was meant to be. *I hope she does not look at the scar and remember the old me.* She stays fixed on my eyes. We embrace. I squeeze tight.

"My Maeko," I murmur, the tremble of my voice clearing.

I hold tight, not wanting to let go. She squeezes me. Tears roll down my face without any shame as others watch.

"I'm taking you home, Papa," she says, with her voice rasping as if she's been crying for days. A warm tear drops off her cheek onto my neck, providing a sensation greater than any raindrop.

***

After the swell of our emotions settles, Maeko explains. "Atsuko called and said you're still alive and that you found me through my music CD. I told her you died in the war. But now I know it's real. It's really you."

"I never heard from Atsuko," I tell Maeko.

"She offered to fly to the Philippines to get you, but I told her I would go. I think she's quite fond of you, Papa," she says, looking for my reaction. In the comment, I know that Tamiko is gone.

Afraid to hear the answer, I ask, "And Mama? What happened to your mother?" I brace my emotions.

Maeko grabs my wrist.

"I'm sorry, Papa," she says, looking at me.

And just like that, as simple as it could be, I let go of the remaining hope for reuniting with Tamiko. *Be at peace, my love.* As if God has given me permission, I think of Atsuko's smile, without guilt, on that day we met in the rice field.

Maeko tells me that she survived the atomic blasts only because she moved to Hatsukaichi for her education at Nippon Preparatory Academy for the Arts, while Tamiko was commissioned into labor by the government manufacturing munitions in Hiroshima. I look deep into Maeko's eyes to read how heavy the burden was that she did not have her mother or father all those years.

"Tell me more," I prompt her.

We sit, and she describes a good life with the support of Tamiko's parents.

"But there was always a void in my heart," she tells me. "My music kept my hopes up."

"Hope that we would be reunited?" I ask.

"Hope that I would find out what happened to you," she tells me. "I never imagined you'd still be alive." She grabs my hand tight. "It's a blessing, Father."

I'm sorry, is what I wish to say. *I'm sorry for leaving,* I think, as I squeeze her hand and stare into her eyes. Instead, I ask, "Your music? The shakuhachi?"

Maeko's smile grows.

"Oh, Papa. I'm so happy I'll get to play for you. It's my life, my passion, and fortunately, it's my career."

When Manny finds a shakuhachi for us later that day, we sit together on the steps of my porch with the neighbors gathered around. She adjusts her lips onto the instrument and raises her arms to play. I prepare to slide away to give her space, but releasing one of her hands from the shakuhachi, she grabs my arm.

"Stay," she says.

There's a lull of silence when she closes her eyes, as if to transcend our world. She starts in a soft tone, much like the first chirps of evening crickets, and when she reaches a crescendo, my eyes well up, recognizing the melody as the same melody that stayed with me during my time marooned in the jungle. She finishes the song and looks over to me to see the gloss in my eyes. She smiles. But little does she know it's much more profound than a father hearing a daughter play for the first time.

"Beautiful," I tell her. "The most beautiful thing I've ever heard."

I've seen the worst and seen the best humankind has to offer. I've seen the worst and best I have to offer. Those years marooned were a necessary path for my life, with all scars now healed. I chose to forgive others and chose to forgive myself with no remaining doubt over the greater force at work. While I'm reeling from the emotion of the performance, Maeko says, "I'm flying you home, Papa. You're safe now," choosing not to see that scar across my cheek.

THE END

About the Author

American author C.M. Dinsmore has lived and studied abroad. He continues to explore the world, challenge himself, meet a wide array of people, and find spiritual resonance in the things he does while carving out a niche in literary world. CM encourages readers to follow and engage with him via his website.

Please contact the author or publisher for comments, inquiries, or to report errors.

Errors can also be reported directly on most Kindle devices.

More about author: www.cmdinsmore.com

More about publisher: www.heliotropic.media

Did you enjoy my novel? If so, please leave a review at one or more of the many book sellers or book related websites.

www.ingramcontent.com/pod-product-compliance
Lightning Source LLC
LaVergne TN
LVHW031336150826
845673LV00012B/2923

* 9 7 8 1 9 6 1 4 2 1 0 0 4 *